Charlotte

Kate Petty was born in 1951, the youngest
of four children. Her own teenage years were
spent at a coeducational boarding-school,
before going on to York University. She
divides her working life between publishing
and writing. She lives in London with her
husband and teenage son and daughter.

The Girls Like You Quartet

Sophie
Hannah
Maddy
Charlotte

Charlotte

KATE PETTY

Dolphin Paperbacks

These books are for Rachel, who approved

First published in Great Britain in 1999
as a Dolphin paperback
by Orion Children's Books
a division of the Orion Publishing Group Ltd
Orion House
5 Upper St Martin's Lane
London WC2H 9EA

A catalogue record for this book is
available from the British Library

Typeset at The Spartan Press Ltd,
Lymington, Hants
Printed in Great Britain by
Clays Ltd, St Ives plc

One

On the last day of the summer term we had a sleepover at Sophie's. Mum would've let me have it at our house if I'd wanted, and there's plenty of space at Hannah's, but we usually end up at Sophie's. Anyway, Sophie has the whole loft to herself with her own bathroom and TV, so it's no problem for her to have three extra. In fact, Sophie's pretty cool altogether – nothing seems to be much of a problem for her, as far as I can see.

Which is not true in my case! I'm Charlotte. I've got boring light-brown hair and I'm a bit fat with a big bum. 'Baby-faced' is how my sister describes me, and that's being kind. I think she was quite tubby too when she was my age, but now she just constitutes yet another of my problems. Michelle is sixteen and stunning. When the phone rings it's always for her. Michelle finished her exams weeks ago and now she's in Corfu with her friends – 'recovering'. Oh yeah. I end up doing all the chores, being on the receiving end of all Dad's sarky comments about teenage girls (laziness thereof), even though I'm doing the work of both of us and feeding her hamster and her cat as well as my own. If I'm telling you about

1

myself, which I seem to be at the moment, I should add at this point that I'm soft about animals. I certainly won't eat them – much to Mum's annoyance – or use anything that's been tested on them. And animals like me. They don't care how fat or thin you are. If only it was the same with boys.

Back to the sleepover. There are four of us who have been friends since primary school. Hannah's gone to an all-girls school but she lives near by and still spends her free time with us. Hannah and I are both quite shy so we get on well, but she's known Sophie even longer because they live close to each other. And then there's Maddy. Maddy is in a totally different league from me, as you'll see. In fact I do sometimes wonder why they include me – I'd die rather than be a hanger-on. I expect it's because I make them all look gorgeous and slim by comparison!

I was the first to arrive at Sophie's. Sophie's older brother Danny opened the door. He usually says hello, but today he just bellowed up the stairs, 'Soph!' and disappeared back where he'd come from, leaving me standing in the hall blushing furiously. To be fair, he'd just had a terrible haircut – perhaps he was making himself scarce. Sophie appeared at the top of the stairs. She'd changed since school into tiny shorts and a skinny top which had the usual effect of making me feel enormous in my baggy T-shirt and jeans. Instant inferiority complex kicked in . . .

We went to sort out the food. Whereas my mum is big on home cooking, Sophie's is happy to buy all the stuff we actually like. Pizzas, loads of crisps and dips, salad that probably wouldn't get eaten, bottles of juice and Coke were laid out on the big table in the kitchen. Sophie slapped my hand as I scooped up some cream-cheese-and-chive dip with a dorito, 'Oy! Don't be piggy! We're taking this lot upstairs. Carry some bottles!' At that point, the doorbell rang.

Sophie opened the door and Maddy made an entrance. 'Hi guys!' Maddy addressed the world at large and kissed us both, enveloping us in a wave of her latest scent – which actually I can't stand – but you can't help liking Maddy. She spotted Danny behind the door (where had he come from?), ruffled his hair and said 'Like your hair, Dan,' before he had time to run and hide again. Mum and Michelle describe Maddy as a 'luvvie', and I'm sure she will end up on the stage one day. She's shorter than Sophie, but taller than me, with browny-gold hair, a terrific tan, good cheekbones and browny-gold eyes with long, curling eyelashes. Sophie is cool, but Maddy, as everyone knows, has something else. Sex appeal, I suppose.

Hannah arrived last. She is a very different kettle of fish from the other two. We definitely all like her, but it's hard not to feel a bit sorry for her. She's dark and intense. She used to have a funny way of walking (I don't notice it any more), which is why she's known as 'Duck'. Her parents both work and expect her to do really well at school but they don't seem to care much about her otherwise. Hannah peers through her glasses and always seems anxious about something. Actually she can also

3

be very funny in a quiet, dry way, but in our group you have to listen hard to hear her.

Sophie's loft is brilliant. It feels cut off from the rest of the house. She'd laid out mattresses for us round the edges with the TV and video at one end. We put the food and drink in the space in the middle and made ourselves comfortable for watching the video – a faithful old horror movie that we could all scream along to. 'Shall I set the vid going, Soph?' asked Maddy, who was closest.

'No, let's wait for my brother to go out first' said Sophie. 'I'll put some music on.' Sophie prides herself on having the latest CD, and usually the T-shirt to go with it. Maddy tends to follow her lead, and so do I. But Hannah, who's really brilliant at classical stuff – she plays the flute and the piano – is often the first to hear a band and tell us about it. Somehow, because Hannah's not a cool person like Sophie and Maddy, we forget that she's got great taste.

Sophie and Maddy went into their usual dance routines. Sophie's not such a show-off as Maddy, and you won't catch me dancing in public, but it was fun to watch them anyway, while getting stuck into the serious business of the sleepover – eating. Then Dan went out and we spent the next couple of hours watching Freddie do his stuff. My parents still think I'm too young and impressionable to watch horror movies – little do they know . . . Personally I'm more interested in the food than the blood and gore, and if I'm honest, I do have to look away from time to time. Hannah never seems scared and nothing is too gross or too sophisticated for Maddy and Sophie. I ate a lot of pizza and a very large amount of chocolate fudge brownie, with squirty cream. Well, I know I shouldn't be so piggy, but what's the point, when the only boy I've ever been interested in will never fancy me anyway? All that lot was washed down with 7-Up, Coke, and a sip of the red wine that Hannah said her dad wouldn't miss. Funny how often I fail to catch the end of the video at a sleepover.

Sophie's parents came home and called upstairs at some point to ask if we 'were ready for bed'. I dived into my sleeping-bag to change into my night things – I wouldn't like to offend the others with my bulging flesh (in all the wrong places), but Maddy is more than happy to flaunt herself. Hannah is a sleeping-bag changer too. Sophie does her cool-Sophie thing and gets round the problem by sleeping in the T-shirt and knickers she's wearing. We sat round with cotton-wool balls and cleansers and face packs with the usual late-night TV antics going on in the background. It was great. Sleep-overs are great. It's just so brilliant being up late with your friends. The next bit's even greater. We all snuggled down in our sleeping-bags.

'Wish Ben Southwell was here . . .' began Maddy.

'That little jerk?' said Sophie, a tad viciously. 'I'd rather have Leonardo di Caprio.'

'Louis Armstrong! John Lennon!' squeaked Hannah.

'They're dead,' shouted Sophie, drowning out my 'Josh Rowlinson, please, God.'

'Oh, well,' said Maddy, 'if we're talking real men here,

give me . . . give me KEANU! I was just talking – attainable. Anyway, Ben's cute!'

'Too young!' said Sophie. 'All the boys in our year are too young. They're titchy.'

'Ben isn't,' I said. I thought he was pretty cute myself. And most people aren't that titchy compared with a short-arse like me.

'Well he's not too short for you, Charlotte,' said Sophie, 'but you've got to admit he's too immature for us. And anyway, he kisses like a fish.' Before we could all ask her what she meant by that, she asked me, 'What about your loverboy in Cumbria – Josh thingy?'

I sighed. Josh is so out of the question I don't have any secrets about him. 'He's eighteen, for God's sake.'

'Sounds all right to me,' said Maddy.

'Not when you've got a skinny sister like Michelle it isn't.' The others had to agree with me. Grim as it is having a sister like Michelle, she does sometimes up my street-cred with the group – to my advantage. Suddenly they were all interested in what Michelle was doing, who she was going out with, how she had her hair. I was telling them when Maddy interrupted with her old theme.

'A real man. That's what I want. A real lovey-dovey Mr Darcy of my own. Perhaps I'll meet him on holiday.'

'Well, I'll get to see Josh on holiday—' I said.

Maddy turned her full golden gaze on me. 'Oh really, Charlotte? Oh you're so lucky. Is Michelle going?' she asked crushingly.

'No, just me—'

Now Sophie joined in. 'Well then, Charl – it's your big chance.'

'Fat chance,' I said, 'with the emphasis on fat,' but the others weren't going to be put off. I let them argue it out among themselves. On the whole, Maddy thought I was in with a chance. Sophie and Hannah (who know me and my holiday circumstances a bit better) thought that maybe I wasn't.

'Tell us again, Charlotte,' said Maddy beseechingly. 'I want to imagine it all.' So, pleased to be the centre of attention for a change, I did.

Every summer Michelle and I spend a couple of weeks in the Lake District with my aunt. This very sensibly means that Mum can get on with some work without feeling guilty in the summer holidays and that my aunt, who is a widow with three boys to look after, gets some female company and support. This isn't as ghastly as it sounds because my Aunt Viv is great, the sort of wacky, arty primary school teacher that everybody adores. And it's not like the boys are the seven dwarfs, who need a female about the place to wipe their noses – we just give a hand with the little ones in exchange for a holiday in the Lakes. Their house is in a beautiful place and all the picnics and swimming they do are cool. The boys are Ollie, Tom and Ned, in that order. Ollie's thirteen. Tom's nine. Ned's six. So who's Josh Rowlinson, you ask? Well, my aunt's house is actually half of a big old mill house. The Rowlinsons live in the other half. Little Kate Rowlinson is Ned's best mate, and Joe Rowlinson is Ollie's. And Josh Rowlinson is their eighteen-year-old

7

half-brother who also spends the summer there. I've been madly in love with Josh Rowlinson as long as I can remember. He looks like a young version of Daniel Day-Lewis, kind of saturnine, and doesn't deserve my devotion one little bit. He's never taken any notice of me whatsoever, apart from teasing me once or twice for blushing. Sadly, he started taking notice of Michelle last year.

'But this year, Charlotte,' said Hannah romantically, 'with no Michelle, he's bound to realise what a fantastic person you are, and how kind . . .' She tailed off lamely.

Maddy was off again. 'We'll all have holiday romances! Let's all agree to have holiday romances! And we'll have another sleepover on the last weekend of the holidays and report back. Let's go round and everybody say where they're going. Age order. I'm nearly fifteen – God, would you believe it – so I go first. OK, I'm going to Barbados with my dad. Two weeks. What about you, Duck?'

'Me?' said Hannah. 'Oh, the usual boring old music course with a load of musos in sandals.'

I was shocked. 'But I thought you really liked doing your music. And mightn't you meet a wonderful double-bass player or a sexy saxophonist or someone?' I've always been jealous of Hannah's talent – felt it swept her up into a glamorous world of musicians and artists.

'I might,' said Hannah. 'But I don't promise to talk about it afterwards.'

'Spoilsport!' said Sophie, and we all joined in the jeering. Hannah kept her mouth shut, so Sophie said,

'I'm going to yet another French campsite. With one nerdy older brother. Mum and Dad read and drink and go to museums and markets. I'm left with dear Danny to mingle with all those other campers. I suppose I might just find myself a campsite courier on a bicycle . . . You're so lucky Mads – Barbados! You'll have to have a wonderfully exotic time for all of us.'

'Well, I'm the youngest,' I said. 'But you all know about me.' I fell asleep soon after that and dreamt of Josh.

Two

Four days later I met up with Hannah and Sophie at the shopping centre. 'You all ready to go then, Charlotte? Got your bikini packed?' asked Sophie. 'Hannah and I are going to try some on now.'

'It's not a bikini sort of holiday,' I told her.

'Oh, go on!' said Hannah. 'If I can make a prat of myself, I don't see why you shouldn't.'

'Hannah! Me? In a bikini? You *are* joking?'

'Not really. You're not half as fat as you think you are. I don't think you've noticed that it's dropping off you, have you? Considering how much you eat?'

I was about to thump her, but she said, 'I dare you to try one on!'

'Oh OK, but only if they have fitting rooms with cubicles . . .'

Three heads popped round the curtains of three different cubicles. We all stepped out like synchronised swimmers. 'Ta-da!' Sophie looked great. So did Hannah without her glasses.

'Charlotte, you look OK, really,' said Sophie.

And, though I say it myself, I did look OK. 'It seems to hide a multitude of sins.'

'Buy it!' said Hannah. 'You can seduce Josh in it!'

I conveniently forgot how useless this garment would be for swimming in the icy mountain tarns, and went ahead and bought it. Now I was ready for my holiday.

The train journey to Oxenholme from Euston took three hours and twenty minutes and it poured with rain nearly all the way. My wellies were well to the fore in my luggage. My new bikini was tucked away in a pocket. I had two magazines, a book of horror stories, a Walkman and some sandwiches to while away the time. There wasn't much to see beyond the raindrops on the window and some wet fields. I put on my headphones and let Bob Marley soothe me into a holiday mood . . .

I stepped down from the train in the hazy golden light of evening. The train pulled away and left me standing on my own on an empty platform. I made my way over the bridge and looked around the car park for Aunt Viv's battered Volvo. The cars were all empty. I was just wondering what to do when a crazy orange Beetle skidded into view. The door slammed and a tall, dark-haired guy stood up and seemed to be looking for someone. He kept looking at me and then looking beyond me to the platform. Eventually he came up to me and asked, 'Excuse me, do you happen to know if the London train has arrived yet? I'm meeting a girl—' He stared at me. 'My God, it's you, Charlotte. I didn't recognise you . . . You've changed . . . you look so much older . . .' Josh stuttered to a halt and gazed down at me with his clear green eyes. After a few moments he remembered his manners. 'Here, let me take your bag and you can get in.' I sat in the passenger seat of Josh's amazing car. 'I offered to come and meet you,' he said, starting the engine. 'Viv was really busy getting ready for you and she was still waiting for Ollie and Joe to get back from playing football. I wanted to see you again. I've always wanted to tell you how much more beautiful you are than your sister and when I heard she wasn't coming, I thought this might be my chance. I think it's going to be a wonderful summer . . .'

Hang on! Wake up Charlotte! This is Josh I'm dreaming about? Supercilious, silent Josh? Josh who only recently woke up to the charms of Michelle? Josh, who only speaks to me to tease me and laugh at me blushing? Yup. Oh well. Dream on. The last hour of the journey is always the best. The scenery got more scenic and the weather began to clear. It was still wet everywhere, but at least it was all *green* and wet. I started to feel excited, that great end-of-journey feeling when you can't wait to get there but at the same time you want the journey to go on for ever. Finally we pulled into Oxenholme. I lugged my bags out on to the platform and almost before I'd set them down there was Aunt Viv throwing her arms round me, Ned (my littlest cousin) grabbing my hand, Tom gallantly offering to carry my bags and Kate (Josh's baby sister) hauling on the lead of an overexcited dog. Quite a welcome.

'Charlotte, sweetheart, it's lovely to see you!' said Aunt Viv. 'Ned and Kate have been on at me all day – "'When's she coming? How long till she gets here?'" Tom's changed his meeting-Charlotte clothes about six times, haven't you Tom?' Poor Tom blushed furiously. Just like me. He's always been my favourite.

Viv shepherded us into the car. Scrappy hopped into the back. I'd say hello to her later. Tom was quickly absorbed in his Gameboy but Ned and Kate started telling me about all the expeditions they'd saved for my visit.

'And it's going to be Joe's birthday next week and we're all going to the boathouse to have a party for him. Him and Ollie have been planning it,' said Kate. She looked at me from under her dark fringe with incredibly clear green eyes. (Oh, Josh.) 'Even Josh says he'll come to Joe's birthday,' she added, as though a little kid could read my mind, but then she sent my hopes plummeting with 'though he's not so interested now he knows Michelle isn't coming.' And she and Ned curled up with laughter.

'Josh fancies Michelle!' chortled Ned. 'He'd really like to . . .' but his rude six-year-old sentence was too much for him and he spluttered.

I looked straight ahead and pretended to be above such smutty talk, though from the corner of my eye I could see that Tom had looked up from his Game-boy and was watching me. Even when he was tiny Tom had seemed to understand my feelings about things. He rounded on the little ones and said, 'Don't be stupid. You're just making that up. Of course Josh is coming to Joe's birthday.' He leant forward to me, 'We're going to play Water Warriors. Will you double with me?'

I laughed. Water Warriors is a game to make you forget any airs and graces. We play it nearly every year at the boathouse. It's basically a fight on boats and rubber dinghies and lilos where everyone tries to get everyone else into the water. There are all sorts of complicated rules that keep on changing every year. The only rule that doesn't change is that *everyone* has to play, grown-ups and tinies included. That's why you have to fight in pairs – one strong and one weak or two middlings. I reckoned Tom and I were a good pair of middlings. 'Josh is going to double with me!' said Kate. She's very proud of her big brother. 'Joe and Ollie have been training. They think they can go as middlings, but I think we should split them up. Joe's getting really big.'

'So why weren't Ollie and Joe here to meet me?' I asked Aunt Viv.

'They're a waste of space, socially, this summer,' she said. 'It's all sport, mostly football, for them. You think we'd get a break in the summer, wouldn't you?'

'So what's new?' Ollie and Joe have been hitting a ball around as long as I can remember.

'It's just a shame, since they're closest to you in age.'

'Don't worry about them, Aunt Viv! You're my friend among all these boys. We girls need to stick together!'

'And me,' said Kate from the back, 'I'm a girl too!'

We bumped up the driveway and pulled into the yard of the L-shaped house. I suddenly felt nervous. What if Josh was there? I composed myself to look thin and sophisticated as I climbed out of the car, but then Scrappy jumped up to greet me. 'Hello soppy dog . . .'

'Hello soppy cousin!' There was Ollie in the yard, much taller than last year. 'Come round later, Joe,' he called after another lanky lad – Joe! – disappearing next door. Joe nodded at me briefly before going in – to where Josh was, no doubt. I began to recall just why Aunt Viv was so glad of female company.

'Now you've seen everyone except Josh,' said

Kate. 'And my mum and dad, but they don't count. Can I help you unpack?'

Three

We have a first-night ritual of going down to the weir to watch the salmon leap. The mill house isn't far from the water-mill, which of course is on the river. The river has to be tightly controlled near the mill to make sure there's always enough water to turn the wheel, so there's a whole system of pools and weirs. Every summer the salmon make a fantastic journey to their spawning grounds up the river, swimming against the stream all the time. If they come to an obstacle like a weir they just have to gather all their strength and jump up it. They hurl themselves up the fall of water again and again until they make it. And then you imagine them going on and on, getting more and more exhausted but still driven to get upstream and reproduce. Crazy really.

Aunt Viv stayed behind to cook supper but everyone else came down to the weir – my three cousins, Joe and Kate Rowlinson, and the dog. Kate and Ned swung from each of my hands. Ollie and Joe went on ahead and Tom and Scrappy ran between us. The rain had given way to a beautiful fresh evening with sopping wet grass underfoot and birds wheeling and calling high overhead. If only Josh had come too, it would have been perfect. But then again, I was more relaxed without him around.

We walked past the mill and over the stile into the field that runs beside the river. Each year it's the same – I'm knocked out by sheer pounding force of the river, and the smell of it. Tom was caught between wanting to push on with the bigger boys and being with me. He took it upon himself to report back to us what Ollie and Joe were up to. 'They've gone down the bank . . . ' off he went again. 'They're tightrope walking across the weir . . .' Away again. 'Joe's found a salmon caught in some weeds.' Next bulletin: 'Joe's rescued the salmon! He threw it up to the top and it swam away. Come on, you're missing everything.'

I suddenly realised that Scrappy wasn't with us. 'Tom, where's Scrappy?'

'Oh, nosing down a burrow somewhere. She's all right. There aren't any sheep in this field.' Scrappy is a mongrel with a lot of sheepdog in her. She can't help rounding animals up, whether they're sheep or ducks. It would be hilarious at home but in this part of the world it's deadly serious. She could get shot on sight for worrying sheep. We climbed over the final gate to the weir. Ollie and Tom stood watching. I'd hardly ever seen them so still!

'Charlotte, Joe's a hero,' said Ollie. 'He rescued this fish! It was gasping away and he managed to pull all the weeds free and then he just picked it up ever so gently and popped it up to the top of the weir. Another life saved. Lives probably, think of all those baby salmon.'

The hero was leaning on the fence watching the silver salmon leaping through the tumbling water. 'I'd be too squeamish to hold a fish,' I said to him. 'I'm impressed.'

Joe looked at me intently and I realised for the first time that he had grown way taller than me. He's always been quiet and serious with warm brown eyes and a skin that's quick to flush. It was flushed now. You have to be careful not to tease Joe. 'I'm always impressed by people who are good with animals,' I felt I had to explain. That seemed to satisfy him and he turned back to watching the fish.

'Eleven!' shouted Ned above the noise of the water. 'I've counted eleven fish jumping!'

'I've counted twelve,' said Kate, not to be out-done.

'Well, I've only seen six make it so far,' said Tom, wanting to show that he knew what he was talking about.

'Yeah, it's six,' said Joe, and Tom looked pleased because Joe certainly knew what he was talking about.

'Where's Scrappy?' asked Ollie after a while.

'Looking for rabbits,' said Tom.

'That dog'll get herself shot if you're not careful,' said Joe. 'We'd better find her.'

Ollie looked at Joe, surprised. 'What, now?'

'Yes. You lot just can't seem to get it into your heads that sheep-worrying is a big deal round here. It's farmland, not a park. Let's find her. Dad said the other day that old Blaythwaite on Upper Farm was complaining about dogs worrying the sheep. He wouldn't know that Scrappy was just trying to round them up.'

We set off for home, calling Scrappy as we went. Sure enough, she was bounding through the brambles that edged the first field, pretending to chase rabbits.

'We needn't have worried, Joe,' I said as Ollie called Scrappy to heel.

'It's better that we did,' said Joe, and turned that intense brown gaze on me again.

After supper I bathed Ned and read him a bedtime story. Tom, who'd given up his bedroom for me, snuggled up to listen too. 'I'm glad you're here,' he said. 'Ned and Kate are too little for me and Ollie and Joe are too big. You won't stop doing things with me when Josh comes along, will you?'

'Why ever should I do that, Tom?' I asked innocently. Why indeed, when every minute since I'd arrived I expected Josh to materialise. I couldn't get him out of my mind, especially when it was quite possible that he *might* walk in at any time. Even here, in Tom's bedroom, I didn't feel safe.

'I just thought you might, that's all.'

'Don't worry, Tom. You know we're cool.' I wasn't sure I could reassure him any more than that.

When I got downstairs the TV was on and three large male figures were crouched over it. That meant Ollie and Joe – and Josh. See what I mean? None of them looked up when I went in. My heart started to thump because of Josh being there but I went into the kitchen to seek refuge with Viv.

'Take this tray of coffees into the boys, would you, love? There's one for you there and I'll come and join you in a minute.' I wasn't to be spared after all. My hands were trembling so much that the mugs shook and coffee spilled all over the tray.

'Ah, great,' said Ollie and reached out for his drink. Josh followed suit without even looking up.

'Thanks, Charlotte,' said Joe.

I took my coffee and perched on the only available seat, on the sofa between Ollie and Josh. 'Eugh! No sugar!' said Ollie and stood up suddenly. I was catapulted backwards, shooting my coffee into Josh's lap. I've never seen anyone move so fast! Josh certainly noticed me then.

'Stupid cow!' he yelled.

'I'm sorry,' I said.

'So you should be,' growled Josh, dabbing at himself with tissues.

I noticed Joe grinning nervously up at me. Ollie, whose fault it was really, finally came to my defence. 'That's no way to speak to my cousin, Josh.' But it was too late. Josh's trousers were soaked and he was going home. It was quite obvious that in his eyes I was nothing more than a stupid girl, no – worse, a stupid cow. Probably a fat cow, too.

So that, as far as my holiday romance was concerned, was clearly that.

Four

When I woke up next morning it took me a while to get my bearings. Ah yes! Lake District. With Josh, the love of my life, only a stone's throw away. And no Michelle. I hoped everyone wasn't too disappointed that it was only me this time. There was a gentle tap on the door and Tom came in with a cup of tea for me. Though most of it was in the saucer he was very pleased with himself for bringing it and plonked comfortably on the bed to tell me about the day ahead.

'Ned chose today. We're taking a picnic up to Black Gill. It's his favourite place.'

Black Gill was one of my favourite places too. It's high up in the fells with a pool deep enough to swim in and nothing and no one but sheep for company.

'It's just us. The Rowlinsons are going into town with their mum.'

I wasn't sure whether to feel sorry or glad about this news. On the whole I think I was glad.

Ollie washed up after breakfast while Viv and I put a picnic together. 'I hope you don't feel too grand for picnics and swimming, Charlotte,' said Viv, filling a Thermos.

'Of course not! To be honest, it's quite a relief to be able to do all these things without worrying what my friends would think. They can't quite get to grips with the concept of a holiday without a sun tan! Bit like Michelle these days. Though she's still keen to come up after Corfu, even if it is only for the last weekend.'

'That's OK then. So you're not missing her?'

'Not a bit. Michelle's quite bossy – you might have noticed!'

Viv laughed. 'You forget. I've got a big sister too – your mum. You and I have quite a lot in common!'

It was a nice way of looking at things. Especially as I always think of Viv as the tough one. That could be because Mum's always had Dad to share the load, whereas Viv has coped on her own since the boys' dad was knocked off his bike and killed. Ned was still a baby. Viv's not a bit sentimental. I forget she's a widow because she never refers to it. And the boys never seem to feel sorry for themselves either. I really can't imagine being that strong myself.

Aren't other people's families complicated? And that was just my relations! Later that day I was to learn more about the Rowlinsons – and they made Viv's lot seem very straightforward.

The sun was out and great cloud shadows billowed across the fells. I could sense Viv enjoying herself as much as we were. We drove round the curve of a hill and then along a bumpy track that stopped at the gate of a field with a spectacular view across the valley.

'Get that dog on her lead, Ollie,' said Viv. 'There are a lot of sheep about.'

'Poor old Scrappy,' said Ollie as he grabbed her collar. 'Here, girl. Sometimes the sheep are on the other side and she can just run around – but not today.'

We climbed over the gate and carried the picnic stuff and our swimming gear to the stream, scrambling down over the rocks to a sheltered stony beach right by the waterfall. We tied Scrappy's long lead to a tree. 'Swim before food,' said Viv. I wasn't that tempted. 'You can swim again later,' she added, but the boys had already stripped off and were testing the water.

Our little pool was fed by a waterfall. It was about a metre deep – just right for Ned – and roughly four metres in diameter. Ollie went in gingerly but Tom jumped in from a rock and emerged to announce that it was fine, not cold at all, even though Ned, sitting on the next rock and dipping his feet in was already shivering visibly. Not to be outdone, Ollie dunked himself and pulled Ned in and they all splashed around saying how it was quite warm really.

'Men!' said Viv, smiling fondly at her brood. 'Put them in a group and they're all the same, whatever their age. 'So competitive! Just won't be beaten.'

'Look at me! Look at me!' shouted Ned. 'I'm swimming!'

'So what—' Tom began saying, but Ollie leapt on him and shoved him under. And so it went on. I liked watching them. They're quite alike, each one a younger version of the next. Tom is probably the one most like me physically, fairer and a bit more fleshy than the other two. They're very at home in the water, completely unselfconscious, which was why I felt so comfortable with them. I realised how different it was going to be when the Rowlinsons were with us. I couldn't even *imagine* baring my flesh in their presence, not that it ever seemed to bother Michelle. I seem to remember her prancing round Josh in a bikini at every possible opportunity last year.

When Ned was completely blue and even Ollie was shivering, Viv called them in. She threw a towel for me to wrap round Ned and rubbed a squirming Tom down herself. Poor little bundle. 'Come on, Ned,' I said, 'Soon have you dry, and then you can have some soup.' We peeled off his swimming trunks and pulled his clothes on over his damp, goosepimply body. I suddenly had a vision of my friend Maddy in Barbados and smiled to myself. Not glamorous, I thought, but fun all the same. Ned poked his tousled head through the neck of his sweater, normal colour restored to his cheeks. Tom was hopping about trying to put on his underpants without exposing himself. Ollie was expert at doing this under a towel. I averted my gaze and started unpacking the picnic.

'Be good if Joe was here,' said Ollie. 'We could follow the stream up the hill and build a dam.'

'You could do that with me,' said Tom, slighted.

''Spose so,' said Ollie. 'But Joe's older.'

'Well, I'll be ten soon.'

'Big deal,' said Ollie. 'Joe will be fourteen next week.'

'Fourteen?' I asked, surprised. I always thought he and Ollie were the same age.

'Yeah. I'm just thirteen but he's nearly fourteen. The Water Warriors party. Remember?'

So Joe was only a couple of months younger than me then. And I'd never realised. Though I could tell you to the day how much older than me Josh was.

'Let me follow the stream up the hill with you after lunch, Ollie. Please,' pleaded Tom. 'Can we Mum? We could take Scrappy.'

'I don't see why not,' said Viv. 'You could let her off the leash when the stream goes through the field beyond the wall. I don't think there are any sheep up there.'

So after we'd eaten, the two older boys and Scrappy set off. Ned wanted another swim, and as the day was warming up I thought I'd be brave and go in with him once the food had gone down. Feeling distinctly underdressed, even in my regulation black swimsuit, I remembered how cold the mountain water was. Was I crazy? No. This was what Lake District holidays were about, and I'd better toughen up fast.

My swim lasted for all of four minutes. Ned's didn't last much longer. I rather wished I could ask Aunty Viv to wrap me up in a big towel and dry me, too, but I'm a big girl now . . . I retreated behind Ollie's bush to try to replace my wet swimsuit with dry underwear under cover of a large T-shirt. Afterwards I stretched out on a sun-warmed rock with a mug of tea from the Thermos. It was heaven. Ned went down to throw stones in the water leaving me and Viv to chat lazily in the sun.

'I gather Josh wasn't too polite last night,' she said.

'I can't really remember,' I lied. 'I suppose he was a bit brusque.'

'There's no excuse for loutish behaviour, but I do feel sorry for him at the moment.'

'Oh?'

'I can't remember how much you've picked up about the Rowlinsons over the years – but here's the story. John and his first wife split up very acrimoniously. John had been having an affair with his secretary (that's Louise, Kate's mother) for some time before the first marriage ended and it actually sent his wife a bit screwy. She's incredibly neurotic anyhow. She was passionate about Josh but never so warm towards Joe who was quite a difficult toddler – no doubt he was picking up on all the bad feeling—'

'I always thought Louise was Joe's mother?'

'No. You see John and his wife finally agreed to take one son each. Louise was all ready to move in and more than happy to humour John by looking after his little boy. She was desperate to have children of her own but it was several years before Kate turned up. Louise is a good mother to Joe, but it's always been a complicated set-up. Josh was quite smothered by his mum most of the time but she'd sometimes just want to get rid of him so that she could have a life of her own. And that's when he started coming back here for his holidays. In fact he doesn't get on that well with John, who's quite tough with him, and he's a bit jealous of Joe – Joe's life seems pretty normal compared with Josh's. And of course, poor old Josh got shoved off to boarding school – which he hated at first – and so on and so on. One thing you can be sure of is that he absolutely adores Kate. When you see him with her you begin to think that maybe there's a human being in there somewhere, poor boy. Right now he's panicking about his A-level results. His mum rang him last night to say how worried she is. She's not prepared to have him at home if he doesn't get in to college. He was telling us a bit about it while you were reading to the little ones.'

'So does my popular psychology tell me that his mum was the stupid cow, and not me?'

'That would seem to be the size of it.'

Just then Tom came running down the hill. 'Mum! We need you. Scrappy's got in with some sheep!'

Viv leapt up. 'Stay with Ned would you? That dog!' She ran off after Tom.

'Joe says Scrappy will get shot one day,' said Ned on the verge of tears.

'No one would shoot Scrappy,' I consoled him, 'She's far too sweet and silly.'

Ned pulled away from me. I was clearly a hopeless townie when it came to dogs and sheep. 'No. Joe's right. He loves Scrappy but he knows that she mustn't be so stupid with sheep. They won't shoot her, will they?'

I realised that I just didn't know. So I was hugely relieved to see Tom racing towards us shouting, 'It's OK! We've caught her!' Ollie and a very grim-looking Viv followed. Viv was gripping Scrappy fiercely by the collar. Scrappy didn't like it but knew better than to fuss because it was clear she was in big trouble.

'BAD dog,' said Viv, hauling Scrappy to the car. We saw her slapping her on the behind and slamming the boot. She came back to us. 'Come on, pack up the stuff. Let's get the wretched dog home.' She caught our disapproving glances. 'She IS bad. Stupid, stupid dog. What are we going to do with her?'

'She was fine until we were coming back,' said Ollie. 'Then we just couldn't catch her. She was off after the sheep in the near field. I was terrified the farmer would come along.'

'Well, he did come,' said Viv. 'I'd just caught Scrappy and it was obvious she wasn't on a lead. She looked guilty as hell and the sheep were all huddled in a corner bleating their silly heads off. The farmer said, "I hope for your sakes that that dog hasn't been worrying my sheep. Because if she has, and I catch her, you know what will happen, don't you?"'

'And we all just smiled weakly at him,' said Ollie. 'It was awful.'

'Yes, but nothing actually happened, did it?' said Tom (bless him). 'I suppose it was time to go home anyway.'

Scrappy whimpered all the way back, and when we went in the house she ran and cowered in her corner. It was quite pathetic. But I could see that Viv was really shaken by the whole episode. 'From now on,' she said, 'that dog goes on a lead. Always.'

Ollie and I cooked pasta for supper while Viv sat in front of the TV with a stiff drink. She'd cheered up by the time we'd eaten, though, and I even saw her giving 'that dog' a hug before she went to bed.

Five

Only in the Lake District can it rain as it did the following morning. The world outside the windows was a green and grey blur. I came down late for breakfast – Viv had cleared the table and it seemed that the day was well under way. 'No rush. The others are all next door playing on the computer,' she said to me. 'I'm going to the supermarket with Tom and dropping Ollie and Joe at the sports centre. Josh is looking after the little ones.' Even the sound of Josh's name made me feel slightly dizzy. 'Come shopping if you want, but if I was you I'd make the most of the peace and have a lazy breakfast followed by a long bath. There's plenty of hot water. Just make yourself at home.'

I had to admit that it sounded irresistible. 'I'm persuaded,' I said, and Viv went out into the rain.

While the bath was running I dug out my make-up bag from the bottom of my suitcase where it would probably have languished all holiday. Viv had some gorgeous designer shampoo and conditioner and Mum had treated me to a Bodyshop basket of bath oils, so I spent a blissful half-hour in their great deep bath tub. The bubbles conveniently hid my wobbly bits from view – I could even pretend I was lean and fit. I lay there soaking and fantasising about Josh. I wondered when I'd next see him. Would he be nicer this time? Or would he look at me as if I'd just crawled from under a stone? We'd got off to such a bad start.

I only got out when my fingers started to wrinkle. There were warm towels in the big airing cupboard. I wrapped one round me and another round my hair like a turban and padded to the bedroom where I put the radio on full volume. Now all I needed was a hairdryer and I was pretty sure Viv kept one in the drawer in the kitchen. I was just fossicking around down there when the back door flew open with a crash. Ned and Kate rushed in from the wet yard, closely followed by – Josh!

Well, I blushed. Under Josh's sardonic gaze I blushed from head to bare shoulders to bare legs to bare toes. I blushed all over, rooted to the spot before I finally turned tail and shot up the stairs into the bedroom and shut the door, blocking out Ned's cries of 'Charlotte! We've come to play Pictionary. Will you play with us?'

I stayed in the bedroom for what seemed like forever. I brushed through my tangled wet hair and dressed. I mucked about with make-up. Finally I turned the radio off and listened. It sounded quiet downstairs. They'd probably gone back next door. I crept down to the kitchen to look for the hairdryer again and reached for the kettle to make myself a cup of coffee.

'The kettle's on already,' said a voice from the

depths of the armchair. 'They won't play Pictionary until you join us so I've stuck them in front of the TV.' Oh God. Josh is one of those awful silent people who can be there without you knowing. My heart was knocking and I couldn't think of a thing to say. I could feel a major blush creeping up my neck to my face. Then he said, 'And Ollie says I owe you an apology for last night, so . . . sorry if I was rude but if a guy's already in a foul mood and someone pours scalding water on his genitals you can't be too surprised if he's not particularly pleased to see you.' I was completely beetroot by now and utterly beyond speech. I looked at the floor. After a while I glanced up at Josh to see that he was grinning. 'You shouldn't have bothered with the blusher,' he said. 'Here's some coffee, kiddo. Come and play Pictionary.'

How do you *deal* with someone like that?

'I want to play with Charlotte!' said Ned.

'Well, I want to play with my favourite little sister,' said Josh, picking Kate up and swinging her on to his lap. 'Can you play Pictionary with only two people on each side?'

'Easy,' said Ned. 'I draw and Charlotte guesses and you draw and Kate guesses and then we swap.'

'O-*kay* . . .' said Josh. 'Let's go.' He threw the dice and moved his counter on to D for difficult. I picked a card from the box and gave it to him. It said 'boiling water.' Very apt after our recent conversation. I hoped Josh wouldn't mention it. He drew a kettle, made lots of steam come out of it, then drew another picture of the kettle pouring into a mug. All very innocent.

'Boiling water!' shrieked Kate. She was an old hand at this. 'My go! My go!' She landed on A for action. 'I don't understand what it says. What does this word mean, Charlotte?' It said 'clone,' for heaven's sake.

'I think we'd better find you another one,' I said.

'That's not fair,' said Ned, on his mettle.

'It's all right, Ned, I'll do the same for you,' said Josh. Ned was mollified. I couldn't cope with this gentle side of Josh.

It was short-lived. So what did I get to draw? 'Behind.' Josh smirked as he handed me the card. 'I can't draw this!' I was blushing all over again.

'Course you can. Ned sure as hell knows what it is.' I tentatively drew a circle with a line through it. 'Come on Ned, Charlotte's got a big one!'

'BUM!' squealed Ned.

I think the tears came to my eyes at that point. 'Josh! You've made Charlotte cry,' said Kate, all feminine outrage.

'Ah diddums,' said Josh, and put his arms round me, though I was stiff with embarrassment. 'Can't you take a joke then?'

That's when the others came home. 'Why are you hugging Charlotte, Josh?' asked Tom. Viv gave me a funny look. So did Ollie and Joe.

'I expect he's apologising to her,' said Ollie to Joe. But Joe had gone.

'I'm not sure that game was going anywhere,' Josh told Viv without looking at me. 'I'd better give my lot lunch. See you all later.' And he steered Kate out of the back door.

We all helped unpack the shopping. 'So what's on the agenda for later?' I asked, fearing the worst. If the love of my life was to be included I could count on feeling confused and uncomfortable.

'Ollie and Joe want to watch the athletics on TV,' said Viv, 'so I thought we'd take the little ones – and Tom – ' she added, 'to the cinema. They've got the new Disney on. It's really too wet to try and do anything else today.'

It was after the film that I finally got my longed-for ride in Josh's Volkswagen. Not that I really wanted it. Well, of course I did, but I knew I couldn't handle it. I'd sat as far away from him as possible in the cinema, but now Kate and Ned wanted to go with Tom in Viv's car and Josh had the effrontery to ask if I would keep him company in his. I was still furious with him. My relationship with him this year was turning out differently all right. A voice in my head was screaming *Stop playing with me*, but I was incapable of saying it out loud, so I sat silently as he drove us home. We pulled up in the yard. He turned to me in the semi-darkness of the wet late afternoon. 'Don't mind me, little girl.' He rolled his eyes and pulled a terrible face. 'I'm just a crazy guy,' he said in a Hannibal Lecter voice. 'And when's your delicious big sister coming to join us?'

'For the last weekend,' I said flatly. When I got out of the car I had the distinct feeling that someone had been watching us.

Six

'My expedition today,' said Ollie. 'The forecast says it's going to get warm. It'll need to be where we're swimming.'

'Oh no,' I said. 'Not the bottomless tarn with the killer pike?'

'That's the one.'

'So who's coming this time?'

'No Josh, so we've only got the one car.' (Phew. Relief overcame disappointment.) 'We can all fit in if we leave Scrappy behind.'

'Picnic?'

'Me and Tom are doing it with Mum.'

'Swimming things?'

''Course. They're all dry.'

'Anything for me to do?'

'Nope.'

I made myself a cup of coffee, found a magazine

and a hairbrush and curled up in the window seat. My hair is long and thick. When it's clean and I've got it brushed out for a party or something it's possibly my best feature, even though it's a boring colour. Usually, and especially on this sort of holiday, I have it pulled back into a ponytail. Yesterday's rain had made it very scraggy, so I needed to get the tangles out. It could be a long job.

The weather was cheering up. The sun broke through the clouds and streamed through the window, catching the steam of my coffee. I could feel its warmth on my hair. The back door opened and in came Ned and Kate followed by Joe.

Kate ran over to me. 'Oh Charlotte, can I brush your hair?'

'My cousin looks like a princess, doesn't she,' said Ned fondly, 'with her hair all loose?' and the two of them scrambled up beside me. I grimaced at Joe as one of them tugged at a knot. He said 'Hi!' gruffly, and sat down with his hands in his pockets. He couldn't sit still. Scrappy came in and flopped down on his feet with a sigh. Then she looked up at him soulfully.

'You know she's not coming today,' I said.

'That's because she's naughty,' said Ned.

Joe consoled her. 'Aah. Poor old girl. Who's a lovely girl then?' Scrappy rolled onto her back. 'Who's a terrible old flirt then?' said Joe, tickling her tummy. Scrappy whimpered with pleasure.

'She never does that for me,' said Ned, climbing down from the window-seat.

'That's because you're not good with animals like my brother,' said Kate, still combing my hair.

'No, Kate,' said Joe, 'It's just that Scrappy thinks I'm sexier than Ned, don't you Scrappy?'

Ned giggled and rolled on the floor by Scrappy. 'Do you think I'm sexy, do you think I'm sexy . . .'

Kate pulled my hair back and piled it on top of my head for effect. She regarded me seriously and then spoke over her shoulder to the boys. 'We think you're both disgusting, don't we Charlotte? Look, you two, haven't I made her beautiful?'

'Oh yes,' said Joe and headed for the kitchen, Scrappy and Ned in hot pursuit.

The long, blue-black tarn lay before us. It can't really be bottomless, but it's very still and mysterious and there are certainly pike in it because John Rowlinson has caught them there. 'Come on Charl, Joe,' said Ollie. 'Real swimming for mature people takes place over here,' and he and Joe led the way to some rocks further down.

The boys stripped off to their shorts. Ollie waded in and started swimming very quickly, yelping a bit with the cold. Joe went in more slowly, his arms crossed across his chest, gasping as the icy water worked its way up his legs. I undressed down to my swimsuit and followed.

I felt the sun on my shoulders and back. I hitched

my hair into a topknot as Joe looked back at me and called encouragingly, 'It's not so bad once you're in!' He struck off in an erratic crawl to catch up with Ollie. I waded on determinedly until the bottom fell away under my feet and I was forced to get my shoulders under and swim. The water was achingly cold but silky. If I kept thrashing about it became quite bearable and then suddenly it felt fine, amazing in fact. The boys were swimming towards me, Ollie looking tousled and faintly ridiculous, Joe sleek as a seal. I rolled onto my back; it was blissful with the warm sun on my face and the cool water all around.

The boys were swimming towards me but they disappeared suddenly. I felt little nipping sensations on my legs – 'Hey!' Ollie emerged at my shoulder, water streaming from his grinning face. 'Watch out for pike!' he said and Joe also burst up through the surface, his expression all innocence.

'Pigs!' I yelled, but they had gone again. Ollie popped up a few yards in front of me. Where was Joe? I felt vulnerable. More nips, on my feet this time. 'Joe?' Suddenly there he was, right next to me, hair plastered to his head. He shook it out of his eyes and looked at me, water clinging to his eyelashes. 'I'll protect you Charlotte. You just tell me if those nasty pike are nipping you.' And he was gone again, with scarcely a ripple.

'Joe!' I yelled.

'You called?'

'Joe . . . I—' I tried to turn in the water, but something was tugging at my feet, my feet which were miles from the bottom. I felt genuinely frightened, out in the middle of the lake. Ollie was a dot in the distance, and Joe was nowhere to be seen. 'Joe,' I called. 'Help!'

Joe was there, in front of me this time. 'Ha! It was you, wasn't it? Grabbing my feet! You toad!' I tried to splash him, but the water was too deep for me to get any purchase. 'Can we go in now? You've had your little joke. I'm cold. I've had enough.'

Joe was grinning broadly as he ducked and spluttered. 'I thought you'd never ask. Can I practise my life-saving skills on you? Lie you on your back? Tow you home?' He swam behind me, ready to save my life.

'Oh, go on then.' I was feeling rather weak. I turned onto my back. Deftly, Joe gripped my head in his hands and pulled it against his chest, kicking out strongly as we set off for the edge. I let myself be pulled along, gazing up at the banks of white clouds and discovering how it felt to be rescued by a knight in shining armour . . . fab.

'Consider yourself rescued,' said Joe when his feet could touch the bottom. I stood in the water and regarded my knight. It was only Joe, Ollie's little friend, except that he wasn't little – he was really quite tall, and dark, with a muscular torso, and . . . perhaps some mouth-to-mouth resuscitation wouldn't have gone amiss either, but Joe had reverted to shy mode and was jogging towards Ollie and the picnic. I felt as if I had somehow missed the moment. Then I felt stupid. What was all this about? Josh was the one I cared about – not his kid brother.

It was quite hot. We ate our picnic still in our towels. Afterwards I felt sleepy and spread my towel on a rock to sunbathe. I shut my eyes and drifted, the shouts and chatter of the others fading into background noise. I could hear the older boys bantering, Viv laughing, the high voices of the little ones, splashing sounds, waves . . . I imagined myself thin as Michelle in my new bikini and Josh lying next to me, the unattainable Josh of my dreams.

'Do you mind if I sunbathe next to you?' Joe's voice was clear. I opened my eyes. I must have dozed right off, the others were all back in the water. I shut my eyes again. Joe settled himself on a nearby rock.

'Good not having to worry about Scrappy, isn't it?'

I hadn't given Scrappy a moment's thought until then. An image of her crestfallen expression as we left floated into my mind. 'Poor old thing. She's just a bit daft. She'd never hurt a flea.'

'Get herself into trouble one day, that dog,' said Joe. 'And that will be sad. We're good mates, me and Scrappy. I could have trained her properly, but your aunt spoilt her rotten. You have to be consistent with animals, you see. They need to know what's

what. It's no wonder dogs find humans confusing.'
He laughed. 'So do I! Give me animals any day. They
don't let you down.'

We didn't say anything for a bit. Then Joe added,
as if there hadn't been a silence, 'Of course, the
people in my family are *very* confusing. Louise isn't
my real mother, did you know that?'

I said nothing and he carried on. 'But she wanted
me, for Dad mostly. I think she wanted me more
than he did. My real mum can't really have wanted
me that much herself, can she? Dotes on Josh,
mind. Drives him mad. But she didn't want me. I
hardly ever see her, you know. Weird, isn't it?'

He sat up. 'Josh is an OK guy, you mustn't mind
him. No fun for him having just Mum and boarding-school. I think he even misses me sometimes.
And he certainly misses Kate. Josh adores Kate. I
expect you've noticed! Everyone adores Kate. She's
the one that makes us a family somehow. I sometimes wonder what we'd do if anything happened
to Kate.'

'Kate's a cool kid,' I said. And then neither of us
spoke for a while. It had been quite a long speech for
Joe. I felt flattered that he had chosen to tell me
about his complicated family. If only Josh were half
so confiding.

A chilly little breeze whipped up the goose-
pimples on my arms and legs at the same time as I
heard the others approaching. I pulled on my jersey
and jeans, appalled that Joe had been exposed to so

much cellulite, and busied myself with the picnic basket. The little ones were going to need food and hot drinks, fast. Joe went to meet up with Ollie and I didn't speak to him again that day.

Seven

The next day started badly and ended worse than any day I've ever known.

Viv overslept and forgot that Ollie and Tom were doing the football course. They were dozy and she nagged at them in a very un-Vivlike manner to get washed, have breakfast, find their things. Ned got in the way and irritated Tom by playing on his Gameboy without permission. Scrappy kept tripping everyone up. Even I felt like a spare part and tried to keep a low profile. They finally got through the door and Ned and I managed to eat a civilised breakfast, but we were edgy and the day seemed doomed from the start. Not without cause, as it turned out.

Viv returned, sorry about being so crotchety but worried about the car, which had been playing up all the way home and had barely made it up the hill. She had to spend the next hour on the telephone ringing round repair services all without much joy, until she finaly persuaded someone to come out. We sat down for sandwiches and soup at lunch time and the phone went again. Ned, trying to be helpful, answered it, but didn't make matters any better by saying, 'Mum! Here! Quick! Ollie's had an accident!'

Ned and I hung on every word of Viv's half of the ensuing conversation. 'What's happened? Is Ollie all right? . . . Broken? . . . You're not sure? . . . What should I do? I don't know. Which is the nearest Casualty? . . . Oh hell – oh no – I can't come. My car's packed up. I'll have to ask a neighbour . . . I'll be there somehow. Tell Ollie I'm on my way. We'll be there as quickly as we can. Yes, OK. Goodbye.' Then she sat down and put her head in her hands.

'I'll make a cup of tea,' I said, as the only thing I could think of in a crisis. 'Ned, go next door and get Josh. Tell him to come over here – we need him.' Ned was off like a shot.

'What's happened to Ollie, exactly?' I asked Viv.

'It's his ankle. He fell over and landed badly. They think he might have broken it.'

'He might just have a bad sprain. Michelle did that playing hockey. They X-rayed her and everything, but in the end she just had a bandage and crutches.'

'Well, fingers crossed. Poor Ollie. They said he's being brave, but I'm sure it's very painful. Oh goodness, I do hope Josh can get us there. I'm afraid you'll have to wait in for the garage men, and look after Ned and Kate I suppose. I'm so sorry Charl. This isn't any fun for you.'

'Less fun for Ollie,' I said. And secretly I don't mind a bit of a crisis, I think it brings out the best in me. At least, that's what I was thinking *then*.

Josh appeared looking red-eyed and unshaven in a scruffy T-shirt – as if he'd only just got up. I even registered that he didn't look very appealing today. Kate trailed behind him, also looking less than her usual bright-eyed self. 'I've waited all morning for Josh to get up and do something with me', she said, 'and now he's got to go out and leave me. And Mum said we weren't to bother you lot today. She said we spend too much time here and she can't return the favour.'

'Nonsense', said Viv tartly. 'Anyway, Josh is just about to do me a *big* favour, Kate, and you'll be doing Ned another favour by keeping him company this afternoon.' She turned to Josh. 'Thanks, Josh, I'm really grateful. Let's go then.'

'Be good,' Josh warned Kate. He turned to me. 'She's been a right little madam today – don't take any nonsense from her, Charlotte.'

Scrappy saw them leaving and, ever hopeful, bounced after them, nearly tripping them up again. 'No, Scrappy,' said Viv, and 'darned dog – always in the way.' And they were gone.

'Poor Scrappy,' said Kate.

'Well, she does get in the way,' said Ned, unsure

whether to protect his mum or his dog and plumping for his mum.

'Shut up, Ned,' said Kate, throwing her arms round Scrappy's neck. 'It's not my darling Scrappy's fault. She can't help it. Anyway, dogs are much nicer than humans. Aren't they, Scraps?' (Now where had I heard that before?)

'If you're going to be mean, I'm going to watch telly,' said Ned, and flounced off.

'Kate,' I said, perhaps more sharply than I'd intended, 'come on. It's Ollie we've got to worry about, and Viv's broken-down car. I don't want you two squabbling.'

'I'm not squabbling,' said Kate. 'It's been a horrible day. First Mum saying I wasn't to spend so much time with all of you – just because I wanted *her* to stay at home for once. And then Joe going off to have fun and Josh being all grumpy because he didn't want to get up. Josh isn't usually nasty to me, but he was today. And then I am allowed to come here and Ned starts being all unkind too . . .' She put her head against Scrappy's flank, and stuck her thumb in her mouth. I could see that the tears weren't far away.

'Cheer up, Kate. Perhaps we'll all take Scrappy for a walk down by the weir later. Why don't we all—' I was interrupted by a knock at the kitchen door. Scrappy leapt up, barking, and ran towards it. It was the garage men. 'Down, Scrappy!' I shouted, but Scrappy was intent on protecting us from intruders and villains. I opened the door and she rushed out, nearly knocking them over.

'Keep that dog under control, can't you?' said one of the men.

'I'm really sorry,' I said to him. 'Scrappy, get back in!' I grabbed her roughly by the scruff of her neck and shoved her back into the kitchen, shutting the door on her, ignoring the high-pitched barks that came from the other side.

'Where's this car, then? I assume you're not the owner. Got the keys?'

The keys. Viv had them hanging in the kitchen. I'd have to go back in there. I pushed open the door and immediately trod on Scrappy who had positioned herself behind it. She yelped. 'Wretched dog!' I snarled, echoing Viv. I grabbed the keys and tried not to notice Kate's accusing little face as she wrapped herself round Scrappy. 'Won't be long, Kate,' I called over my shoulder, though I don't think she was listening. 'I'm just going to show the men where the car is.'

It was actually a relief to be out of the house, even though it was an untrustworthy sort of day – bright and windy. The two garage men followed me to where Viv had left the car. 'This it?' one asked.

The other guffawed rather rudely. 'More surprising if it *did* go!' he said, kicking the wheel.

I was about to protest, but then the first one pulled himself together and said, 'Don't worry, pet. Could be nowt more'n a dirty plug. At worst it'll need a new fuel pump, and that won't break the bank. Leave it with us. I'll come up to the house when we've sorted it out. Your mum coming back soon?'

'My aunt,' I corrected him. 'I hope so. She's gone to fetch my cousin who's had an accident. They might have to go to Casualty.'

'Fine. Right, let's get a look under this bonnet.' They turned their backs on me and I left them to it.

We always use the back door at Viv's, but the car was nearer the front, so I climbed up the steep, overgrown front path that leads up from the road below. I took my time, savouring the peace. I rang the bell by the front door and waited for Ned or Kate to let me in.

No reply. I peered in at the window of the front room where Ned had been watching television. He wasn't there. I could see the door was open, and I tried to peer down the passage to the kitchen, but it was tantalisingly dark. 'Ned! Kate!' I called. No one came. They don't expect visitors to arrive at the front door. So I set off round to the back again. I passed the garage men bent over the engine, and walked on up to the yard. I was nearly there when I heard Josh's car toiling up the hill behind me. Tom and Joe were with him but no Ollie or Viv. Josh tooted and I waved. My heart started to thump to order. 'That was speedy,' I said.

Josh wound down his window as they drew alongside. He was fully restored to gorgeousness.

'We took them straight to Casualty. Ollie's having an X-ray just in case the ankle's broken. They're in for a long wait though. He's not exactly an emergency. I'll go back and fetch them in a bit.'

They got out of the car and Tom followed Joe into the Rowlinson's house. Josh came with me into ours. I tried to breathe normally. 'Is Kate all right?' he asked. 'She was furious with me earlier on. It probably did her good to be somewhere else for a bit.' I didn't let on that I was worrying about Kate as we pushed open the back door. I'd barely been gone ten minutes. Perhaps she had curled up and fallen asleep with Scrappy in the kitchen where I left her. But Scrappy wasn't there. Nor was Kate. They'd probably gone to watch TV with Ned – except that there hadn't been anyone there either. I went out into the passage. 'Ned? Kate?' The house was silent.

I went back to the kitchen where Josh was filling the kettle, as usual. 'Where are the kids?' he asked.

'Josh, I don't know.' I tried to suppress rising panic. 'When I went out to the car Kate was in here with the dog and Ned was watching telly. Now I don't know where any of them are.'

Josh seemed pretty relaxed. 'Probably hiding somewhere. Let's make them sweat while we have some coffee. I haven't had any breakfast today, let alone lunch.' He passed me a mug of coffee. I took it and sat down in the armchair but quickly stood up because I'd sat on something uncomfortable. It was Scrappy's lead.

'That's OK then,' I said, relieved. Josh was probably right. 'Scrappy's lead is here so Scrappy and the
kids can't be far away.' We sat back with our coffee.
And then we both sat up again and said simultan-
eously—

'—Or Scrappy's out without her lead . . .'

'Oh my God!' I pocketed the lead and ran to the
back door. 'You look for the kids. I have to find the
dog.' I started yelling, 'Scrappy! Scrappy! Here girl!'

Josh raced upstairs and then ran over to their
house. After a few minutes he stormed out to me, as
I stood calling. He was white as a sheet. 'I thought
you were meant to be looking after them. Why did
you let Kate out of your sight? If she's gone after
that crazy dog . . .' The force of his anger made me
reel.

This wasn't the time to argue, or to try and make
Josh stop thinking badly of me. I took a deep breath
and tried to think calmly. What had been going on
when the garage men arrived? Ned had been watching TV in the front room. Kate was with me in the
kitchen. Then the memory of Kate's distressed face
combined with Scrappy's yelps when I'd stepped on
her came back to me: Kate, feeling that everyone
was against her, and poor old Scrappy, who'd been
left behind the day before and shouted at and
trodden on today. I could just imagine Kate saying,
'Come on Scrappy. *I'll* take you out for a walk.' But
why no lead? Even Kate understood about the need
to have Scrappy on a lead. And why would Ned go

too? Perhaps Ned hadn't gone too. Perhaps he'd gone *after* her. And all in such a short space of time.

I ran up the bank behind the house and called again. 'Ned! Ned! Come and help me! I need you!' Then I saw a small dishevelled figure hurtling down from the top of the field in our direction. 'Ned! What's going on? Where's Kate? Has she got Scrappy?'

Ned, out of breath, flung his arms around my knees. 'Charlotte! Where have you been? Kate wasn't in the kitchen when I went in to make friends again. And Scrappy wasn't there either. I called you and you weren't there. I thought Kate had run away so I went up the hill to look out for her. But I couldn't see her . . .'

'Calm down, Ned. I wasn't gone long. I was only out by the car – I wasn't far away. And I'm sure Kate's not far away either.'

'I hope Scrappy's with her. Perhaps she just took Scrappy for a walk. Perhaps they just went for a walk by the weir. I hope Scrappy doesn't pull too hard on her lead – sometimes even Tom can't stop her pulling . . .'

I tried not to think about the fact that Scrappy wasn't on a lead.

Josh was still at the kitchen door. He seemed rooted to the spot. I had to be the sensible one. This might be serious. Ned ran in to Joe and Tom, but they were unmoved by his panic and ambled out to join us. Josh just stared at them, paralysed. 'We've lost Kate and Scrappy,' I explained, 'and I think that Scrappy might not be on her lead.' Joe's eyes widened and I could see him visibly snapping into action. He drew himself up.

'Tom,' he said, 'take Charlotte and Ned over to the weir to look for Kate. She can't have gone far, but the dog could be anywhere. Josh, if you drive back to the hospital now, I'll come as far as Upper Farm with you and then work my way back to join the others. You know what I'm thinking: that daft mutt's a disaster waiting to happen. Send Tom back in a couple of hours to report to Viv. It's still only three-thirty – no need to phone Dad and Louise yet, but we might have to later. Ned, you stay right by Charlotte. And Ned, *think*. Kate's your mate. You know the sort of places she goes. Help Charlotte and Tom, OK? Josh? *Josh*? Come on, get moving!'

But Josh wasn't moving. He looked as if he was about to cry. 'Find her,' he said through gritted teeth. 'Find my little sister. Don't let anything have happened to her. Please God. Just find her and bring her back, and I'll never shout at her again.' He let Joe push him towards his car and they got in.

Tom and Ned turned to me. 'Let's go,' I said. The boys each took one of my hands and we set off for the weir.

The wind was really beginning to get up. The trees shook and rustled and it felt as if rain wasn't far away. Tom was worried and pulled me forward, but

Ned, strangely enough, let go of my hand and danced along behind, talking to himself. Tom said, 'We must find Kate before it gets dark. Just imagine how everyone will be if we come back without her. I'm really worried, Charl.'

'It's ages until then,' I said. 'We'll find her.' We were walking past the water-mill. 'She knows not to go in there, surely?' I asked Ned.

'Kate's not stupid,' said Ned indignantly. 'It's scary in there, she wouldn't go anywhere scary.'

'What if she was looking for Scrappy?'

'Scrappy wouldn't go in there either. Anyway, Scrappy always goes in the brambles here. She's not interested in the mill – no rabbits.'

We walked on, calling Kate and Scrappy all the time. It was getting windier and the sky was darkening, building up to a summer storm. I couldn't bear to think of Kate out here on her own. We went over the stile and into the field by the river. Absolutely everything suddenly seemed hazardous to a little girl and an uncontrollable dog. Could I bear to look in the river? What if she'd fallen in? Tom read my thoughts. 'I'll walk along by the edge of the river. It's not very deep here, but we all know it's fast. We've been brought up by this river. Kate would have been careful.'

' 'Course she'd have been careful,' said Ned. 'Like I said, she's not stupid.' Ned seemed remarkably calm about his friend at this particular moment. Tom went right down by the river below the weir. I could see him squatting down on the bank, pulling back branches and peering into the gloom. Ned held my hand as we watched him.

'What are you thinking, Ned?' I asked him. 'Have you had any more ideas about where Kate is?'

'I'm thinking, Charlotte,' he said. 'I'm thinking, but I'm not scared any more. After all, Kate's older than me, and I wouldn't go in the mill or fall in the river, or any of those things. So I'm still thinking about it.'

I found a big stick for slashing at brambles and long grass. We zig-zagged across the fields. I really didn't know what we were looking for. Perhaps I hoped we'd find a clue, something of Kate's that would tell us where she was. The twenty-minute walk to the weir took over an hour. I hardly wanted to look in the big pools there or under the water-falls. I was scared of what I might find. But Tom was dogged in his search. He crossed right along the top of the weir 'Kate knows we're not allowed to do that,' said Ned, and looked among the trees on the other bank, but there was nothing to be found. We walked on past the weir towards the land belonging to Upper Farm where Joe was. I didn't really know my way round here, and it became increasingly hard to search. As we climbed through Blaythwaite's fields the wind blew cold on us, cutting right through my thin shirt. I tried to concentrate on the job in hand, poking around in hedges, calling, always calling.

There was no sign of Joe. We were all flagging. 'I'd better go back and report, I suppose,' said Tom. 'We've been two hours. Don't worry, I know the way. I'll nip across those fields there. You go back the way we came. Please have Kate with you. I can't bear to think how everyone will be if she's really lost. I can't bear to think how *Kate* will be if she's really lost . . .' He set off at a jog. (And I couldn't bear to think how Josh would be if anything happened to his sister.)

'Can we stop for a bit soon?' asked Ned. 'I've got tired legs and I want to sit down. Can we go and sit on the big boulder by the weir? I don't mind carrying on that far if it's all downhill.' Poor old Ned. I forget sometimes that he's only six. He'd done jolly well.

'Of course. We'll sit down on the boulder and have another good think.'

Tom returned to absolute pandemonium. (He told me all this later.) Josh had brought Viv and Ollie home. Ollie was on crutches, slightly miffed that he was no longer the centre of attention. Viv and Josh were reacting equally badly. Viv, tough Viv, was wailing about her car, her son and her (suddenly) beloved dog. Josh was not helping by saying that it was only a stupid dog that she'd lost. He obviously blamed himself for Kate running off, but he was taking his anger out on everyone else. Tom's arrival without Kate just made everything worse, and they all realised that the Rowlinson parents were going to have to be told. In the end, Ollie said that he would ring them at work, since both Viv and Josh seemed incapable, but in fact there was no need, because John Rowlinson's car could be heard coming up the hill at that very moment. They all stood silently and listened while John went into the Rowlinson's empty house and then made his way next door to them.

'There you are, Josh! Where are the children? I thought you were taking care of everything today?' Of course it was the worst thing he could have said. Josh was rendered speechless, so finally it was Ollie after all who told John about Kate's disappearance. John said angrily that he'd phone the police straight away, he couldn't imagine why no one had done it earlier.

Meanwhile, Ned and I were having our little sit-down. 'Charlotte, Joe said I had to think didn't he?'

'Have you thought some more, then, Ned?'

'Yes. I'm sure Kate's not lost. And I don't think she's hurt herself either. I think she's hiding.'

'*Hiding*?'

'Yes. Kate hides if she thinks people are cross with her. I was cross with her and she probably thought you were cross with her too, as well as Josh.'

Oh God. So it was my fault. 'I wasn't really cross with her, Ned. I just didn't want you two squabbling. I suppose she might be hiding. Where does she like to hide?'

'That's the thing. I don't know. You see, Kate's so good at hiding. She always finds somewhere new.'

We got up and started walking again. We still called for Kate, but I was beginning to feel that Ned might have a point. I hoped he had a point. I much preferred to think of Kate hiding. In fact, that was what Josh had suggested originally. And we hadn't even searched our two houses properly. How crazy! 'Ned, come on, let's get back and make everyone search the house. Josh only had a quick look around, so if she's . . . *hiding* . . .'

As soon as we rushed into the kitchen I felt really stupid. Viv was there. Both the Rowlinson parents were there. The police were there. Everyone was grey-faced. Viv and Josh had obviously both been in tears. I hung Scrappy's lead on the hook on the door where it lived. All eyes were on me. 'We came back,' I said, unnecessarily. 'We thought she might just be hiding.'

Silence.

'Excuse me,' I said, and headed for the privacy of the loo. It was while I was there that I had a sudden thought. Kate liked to trail around after me. Sometimes she followed me to the loo and hung around outside the door, dodging behind a corner as I came out. She was a very sociable little girl. She often kept a conversation or a train of thought going for ages, picking up the threads of what we'd been saying sometimes hours later. I thought about Kate trailing me. What if she'd followed me out to the car? What if Scrappy had followed her?

I whizzed up to my room for a sweatshirt and then slipped out of the front door into the windy evening. Viv's car didn't live in a garage, exactly. She kept it in what was probably once a stable or a pigsty, now almost totally in ruins and hidden by trees. The roof was a sheet of corrugated plastic weighted down with stones. There really wasn't any space around the car in which to hide. The wind rattled the roof and whistled round the old building. A few raindrops bounced overhead.

Suddenly I glimpsed a movement in the car. On the floor behind the driver's seat. Something curled up was curling itself up tighter because I was there. I tried to open the doors. The locks were down. I knocked on the windows. It was too dark in there to see properly. I prayed it was Kate, but I couldn't be sure. I called, 'Kate, it's me, Charlotte! Open the door!' Kate, if it was Kate, didn't move. I realised I'd have to get back into the house, get the keys and get out again, all without raising anybody's hopes. I needed an ally. Who should it be?

Everyone looked up at me expectantly as I went in at the kitchen door again, but luckily the police had just finished making notes and were on their way out. That was taking up the attention of all the adults. I went over to Tom. 'Tom,' I said quietly, 'go and find your mum's car keys and give them to me. I'll be by the front door.'

Tom was amazing. It's quite possible he got the keys from Viv's pocket without her noticing. 'Here. Why do you want them?'

'Because I just *might* have found Kate. I'll slip out the front again. Change the subject if anyone starts asking where I am.'

I went back to the car and opened the door. It was completely dark in there now. 'Kate?' I called. 'Kate? Answer me.' I reached nervously into the corner where I'd seen something and touched a warm body. 'Kate?'

In a tiny voice Kate said, 'Are they all cross with me about Scrappy?'

'Nobody's cross with you, Kate. They're just terribly worried that you've gone missing. Come on, come with me. They've called the police, Kate.'

'Oh no,' she whimpered. 'That's because they're cross with me, isn't it?'

'No, Kate. No one's cross. Just as worried as they could be.' I sat in the front seat. 'Come on. Climb over and have a cuddle.'

She squeezed between the seats and on to my lap. 'You were all cross with me. But I wanted to be with you and I wanted us to take Scrappy for a walk because she was unhappy, so I followed you. I left the door open by mistake and Scrappy came after me.' Kate was tearful. She went on with her story between sobs. 'I tried to get her back in but I couldn't and then I tried to find her lead but I couldn't and then I thought you wouldn't mind her not being on her lead in the garden so I came anyway, but then Scrappy went running off and she wouldn't come when I called her and then I was so frightened that Mr Blaythwaite would shoot her and I knew everyone would be angry with me so I just hid by the wall and then when the garage men left I got in the car. I pressed the button that locks all the doors and I think I must have fallen asleep . . .'

I gave her a hug. 'Let's go back to the house. They'll all be so pleased to see you, Kate.'

Eight

I'll admit that I carried Kate in through the back door partly for effect. I knew how relieved Josh would be to see her. Kate had her arms firmly round my neck and her face was buried in my shoulder. She peeped out at the assembled gathering as they all cried out 'Kate!' and 'Darling!' and 'Sweetheart!' I explained a bit about where I'd found her, but her immediate family were too happy to care about the details. True to form, Kate struggled down and ran over to Josh.

'Don't be cross with me, Josh,' she said. 'Will you read me a story? I want to go to bed now.'

Josh hoisted Kate up into his arms and hugged her very tightly. 'Come on little sis, what shall it be?' It wasn't until they were all in the dark courtyard and Kate was waving goodnight to us over Josh's shoulder that she asked, almost as an afterthought, 'Where's Joe?'

'Joe'll be fine,' said Josh soothingly. 'Come on Kate, let's get you into bed.' And that was the last we saw of the Rowlinsons for a while.

The rest of us reacted quite differently to Joe's absence. 'I don't believe it!' said Viv. 'How could we all have forgotten Joe, even in the heat of the moment?'

'And Scrappy,' said Ollie, gloomily. 'Do you think I ought to go and look for them?' he asked, obviously hoping that no one would say yes.

'Don't be ridiculous!' snapped Viv. 'You can't possibly go anywhere with that ankle.' She looked over at the two younger boys. 'And don't you two think you're going on some wild-goose chase in the dark. It's way past your bedtime! Up you go, all of you. Go on, help Ollie up the stairs!' Slightly shocked by their mother's uncharacteristic outburst, and exhausted anyway, the three boys slunk out of the kitchen door. No sooner had they gone than Viv sat down and started crying uncontrollably.

'Pour me a drink would you?' she asked. 'There's some whisky on the shelf by the videos.' I waited for Viv to talk while I gathered my own thoughts about what to do next.

'Hell! Hell! Hell!' were Viv's first comments on the situation. 'I can't – I just can't hack it.' She heaved some more great sighs, and sniffed. It was very alarming, my aunt behaving like this. 'I think I'm coping, and then I just can't any more! How did this happen? What can the Rowlinsons think of me – two children lost because of one wretched dog?'

'One child found,' I said, 'and the other capable of looking after himself. Don't blame yourself, Viv. None of this is your fault exactly.'

'It is,' she retorted. 'If I'd trained that blasted dog properly none of this would have happened.'

'Look,' I said, nervous that I might end up agreeing with her, 'you've had Scrappy all this time and nothing like this has happened before. You can't help the way the Rowlinsons operate. It's not your fault that Josh and Kate got in a snit with each other, or that Joe takes animals so seriously.'

'Joe!' she said, and started to sniff again. 'That poor child, out God knows where in the dark looking for *our* dog. And you saw how they practically all forgot about him. I just hope that nothing happens to him . . .'

'Viv, Viv,' I tried to comfort her, but I didn't really know what to say.

'I'd like another whisky,' she said, 'but perhaps I'd better just sleep – unless they need me.'

'Go to bed,' I said, though there was no way I could have slept after everything that had happened. 'I'll wait up for Joe. Josh is right, Joe is pretty self-sufficient. I don't think he'll actually be in any danger. But you know what he's like. Once he's started something, he won't stop until it's finished. Go on, go to bed. I'll come and wake you if I need to.'

'Bless you, Charlotte. I'm just about ready to collapse. John will be out searching, that's for sure, so let's hope Joe and Scrappy come back safe and sound. We'll think positive – since there's nothing else we can do. Perhaps they're on their way up the path now.' She went upstairs.

Before long the house was silent. I wondered whether Josh was still awake next door. If only I dared go round there, we could wait together. Huh! I started to make some coffee for something to do. A cup of coffee is the answer to most things in Viv's house. Just then there was a noise outside in the yard. I ran out into the dark – 'Joe?' But it wasn't Joe, it was Josh. Here we go – my heart started pounding away. I was scared of Josh as well as being in love with him. 'Josh? What's going on?'

'I saw your kitchen light on. I hoped you'd be up – I wanted to talk to you.' I couldn't believe my ears. 'Look, sorry I was so unpleasant earlier. Seems like I'm making a habit of it. I was out of my mind with worry. Kind of felt it was my fault. And I took it out on you. When in fact you were the one staying calm.' He stepped over towards me. 'You were brilliant, Charlotte,' he said, and put his arms round me. (Wow.)

'I really didn't—'

'Yes, you did—' he said, and started to *kiss* me, right there in the yard.

'Josh—' I tried to speak, but he wouldn't let me. He was taking this seriously. He gripped my head tightly and his unshaven chin practically grazed my face. I could have started to take it extremely seriously too, if we hadn't been in such a public place. I kept expecting Viv or one of the boys to stick their heads out of the window.

Josh held me close, squeezing my arms to prevent me from resisting his incredible charms. 'Mmmmm . . . I'd never have thought it,' he said dreamily, 'but yes, you're brilliant.'

Brilliant? Me? What at?

'You found Kate. You sorted everyone out.'

Ah. So that's what he was getting at. I pulled away and smoothed myself down, too confused to speak. I'd just been *kissed* by Josh. He turned to go back into his door. 'Better get back – I'm manning the phone. I can't imagine what my little brother's got up to this time.' He punched me lightly on the shoulder. 'We'll carry on where we left off tomorrow,' he said enigmatically. 'Ta-ra,' and he disappeared.

I went indoors and sat down heavily. What's Josh playing at? He sweeps me up in a passionate embrace, leaves me a quivering wreck and then, cool as a cucumber, off he goes. What did he mean, 'We'll carry on where we left off tomorrow'? Heaven only knows. I didn't. And what was all that about? Was that his way of *thanking* me? You're a weird guy, Josh Rowlinson, I thought, but I think I love you. No change there.

I put the kettle on again, still shaking my head in disbelief. I made a mug of coffee and drank it. I switched on the radio. It was after midnight. I dozed off. It was two-thirty a.m. John put his head round the door to say that no accidents had been reported and the police were on Joe's case now, so he was going to try and get some sleep. I passed this information on to Viv, though she barely woke up, but I couldn't go to bed myself. At four a.m. the birds started to sing. I didn't know whether I was coming or going. I kept remembering Josh. I replayed that kiss – rewind, action replay, again, slow motion, fast forward, rewind – until it seemed more like a video than the real thing. Had it really happened? Had Josh really kissed me after all these years of longing? Then I went over the rest of the awful day. I wondered where Joe was.

At four-thirty the sun came up. At five-fifteen I heard the scrunch of stones underfoot. The door was pushed open. I stood up. There was Joe, and in his arms he was carrying a bloody mess that bore a very slight resemblance to Scrappy.

Joe was almost beyond words. 'Towel. On table,' was what he said. I grabbed a clean towel from a laundry basket. Gently he laid Scrappy down. She whimpered.

'Oh Joe—' I started.

But he cut in— 'Boil a kettle and get loads of cotton-wool and some tweezers. And more towels. Quick!'

I switched the kettle on and ran to get my make-up bag. I found tweezers and loads of cotton-wool balls. I brought some extra towels and bandages from the airing cupboard too. Joe spoke softly to Scrappy and stroked her head, almost hypnotising her. 'Hold her while I wash my hands, Charl.' I carried on stroking Scrappy's head. She didn't need holding. She wasn't going anywhere. I hardly liked to look, but I could see that there were two places where the blood was coming from. Why did he want tweezers? Joe put the tweezers in a jug and poured boiling water on them. I realised he wanted to sterilise them.

'No, Joe. Let me boil them in the water in a saucepan, it won't take much longer. You can't take any risks. I've brought some bandages.' I poured some of the water into a bowl and he started to dip the cotton wool balls into it and clean around the wounds. Poor Scrappy looked so weak, almost as if she'd given up. Joe was terribly gentle and kept up a monologue – 'It's OK old girl. We'll make you better. Don't worry. We'll clean you up. I'll get them out.'

Ah, the tweezers. Joe was concentrating so hard he obviously didn't care too much about burning himself as he fished the tweezers out of the water. And I started to realise just what he was trying to do.

'Hold her down, Charlotte. Talk to her. She won't like this but I'll do it quickly. I can see the pellets. And . . .'

I held poor Scrappy down and felt her jerk as Joe inserted the tweezers deftly into the wound and pulled out a pellet. He almost grinned as he got it out. 'There! Just like in the movies!' Needless to say, I was impressed. 'Only seven or eight more to go,' he said grimly.

'What about the other wound?' I asked as he tweaked out the next pellet.

'That's just a nasty cut. It needs cleaning and she'll need antibiotics. It's more important to get rid of this shot right now. She's ever so weak, though. I don't know if she'll make it.'

We carried on the grisly operation until Joe was satisfied that all the shot was out. I counted ten pellets in all. Scrappy seemed more dead than alive. 'Joe, it's after six a.m. Couldn't I call a vet now?'

'How do you propose we get this creature to a vet? They don't do home visits for sheep-worrying dogs you know. Not round here. Not at this time in the morning.'

'Joe, we must tell your family you're safe, anyway. Your dad would drive us? Or Josh?'

'You must be joking!'

'Viv's car's been fixed! Viv will drive us! It's her dog. Please, let me ring.'

I could see that Joe was torn between wanting to save Scrappy all on his own and knowing that she really needed a vet. 'You've done the really important thing,' I told him. 'You got the pellets out. That needed to be done straight away.' I looked at Scrappy. While I'd been trying to persuade him, Joe had cleaned her up some more. He bandaged her leg and lightly covered the shot wound with a swab of cotton wool. Scrappy seemed to be asleep.

'The bleeding's stopped. OK, ring the vet, but I don't hold out much hope. My folks might as well sleep on for the moment.'

I pulled the sofa over and he slumped into it, one hand still resting on Scrappy's flank. I looked at him. He was totally exhausted. His face was grimy and his clothes were muddy and snagged with brambles and burrs. I turned through the Yellow Pages.

'Here's one in the village. Sheila Watson.'

'That's not who they usually go to.'

I had a feeling that a female might be more sympathetic. I dialled the number and waited for the inevitable answer machine. But then a pleasant sounding woman answered. I apologised for ringing so early in the morning and told her what had happened. She listened, interested, and then – I couldn't believe my luck. I gave Joe a thumbs-up sign. 'She's coming!' I said. 'She'll be here in about ten minutes!'

I plonked myself down next to Joe, the sleepless night almost forgotten in my excitement. I looked at his face. Tears were making tracks in the grime. Josh or no Josh, I couldn't help it. I put my arm around him and he leant his head on my chest while I stroked his hair and he stroked Scrappy. Neither of us spoke. We just sat like that until Sheila Watson arrived.

She knocked briefly on the back door and came in with her bag. 'Oh my goodness!' she said as soon as she saw Scrappy. 'I wonder who took a shot at her like that!'

'Joe got all the pellets out though,' I told her as she proceeded to examine Scrappy.

'You did well,' she said. 'Luckily the cartridge only grazed her or she'd have been full of shot and never have survived. Mind you, she'd probably be dead anyway if you hadn't removed the pellets. Your first aid was excellent. We don't want any infection to spread so I'll give her a shot of antibiotics here. She might not last out to the surgery.'

Just then Viv put her head round the door. Viv! I'd quite forgotten to tell her what was going on. And Joe's dad still didn't know he was back. Well, there just hadn't been time. Sleep had revived Viv. 'Joe!' she said, hugging him. 'Thank goodness you're home. Do your family know you're OK?'

'We've been too busy sorting Scrappy out,' Joe said, embarrassed by the hug. 'But I suppose now the vet's here . . .'

'You go home, love,' said Viv. 'You've done more than enough. It's my turn now. You'd better get some sleep, too, Charl. You've been brave and wonderful, bless you both. I'll put a notice on the kitchen door so the boys don't barge in.'

Great, Viv was in charge again.

Nine

It took me a while to get to sleep. It was bright sunlight outside and I could hear the boys getting up and then shushing each other. I could hear their questions – 'Where's Joe? Is Scrappy all right? Why can't we see Charlotte?' I had so many questions of my own. I didn't know where or how Joe had finally found Scrappy or even exactly what had happened to her. We'd been too busy with the 'operation' for questions. I knew that Josh thought I was a heroine but I also knew with far greater certainty that Joe was a hero. I finally dropped off.

It must have been about lunch time when I surfaced. My first impulse was to throw off the bedclothes, leap out of bed and rush downstairs to find out all the news. Then I started remembering the various events of the night. My second, far stronger, impulse was to pull the duvet over my head and stay buried under it for as long as possible.

I thought about Josh. Josh had held me. Josh had kissed me. Josh had been strong and firm and, oh dear, incredibly sexy. Little details replayed themselves – the way he'd wound my hair round his hands to grip my head, the way his teeth had knocked mine, the taste of his mouth . . . Aaaagh! Bury face in pillow time. The way he'd held me so tightly, pinned my arms so I couldn't struggle. What was a girl to do?

And then – Joe. Joe, who once he'd started on something couldn't let it go. Serious Joe who actually *did* things, took action. He must have searched and searched for Scrappy. How far had he trudged for all those hours without ever giving up? How had he felt when he found her? How far had he carried her? And how had he summoned the energy to clean her up and take all those pellets out? No wonder the tears had spilled when it was all over. Then I thought about comforting him, too, and how natural it had seemed. His soft, tawny hair and the tears clinging to his lashes. How he smelt of wet dog (not very pleasant) mixed with the Cumbrian night (gorgeous) . . . Total mindblow, bite the pillow time.

How could I ever emerge from this room? How

could I ever look either of those brothers in the eye again?

There was a discreet tap on my door. It was Tom. 'Charlotte? Are you awake? Mum told me to bring you a cup of tea at two o'clock. Can I come in?' He looked at me expectantly. 'Well? It's all ever so exciting, isn't it? Losing Kate and Scrappy and then you finding Kate and Joe being out all night looking for Scrappy and Scrappy nearly dying. I missed out on all the drama. Joe's been over and told us all about it.'

'You'd better tell me then, Tom, because Joe and I were so busy with Scrappy that I never heard the whole story.'

'Well—' Tom settled himself on the bed and told me what he'd learned about the previous night. Joe's first worry was that Scrappy had wandered over to Upper Farm, Blaythwaite's place. So he started over there, whistling and calling for her and looking in as many fields as he could. But no luck. By eleven o'clock he was starving hungry, so he called into the Ollerton's pub (Pete Ollerton's in his class at school) thinking that he'd buy a sandwich before working his way home. He specifically decided not to phone from the pub because someone else was using it and he knew he'd be home soon. (The grown-ups have all told him off for that!) But while he was eating Joe overheard a conversation that made his blood run cold. A group of farmers were having a heated discussion about summer visitors and dogs. One of them was the farmer from Black Gill. Joe heard him mouthing off about finding some picnickers near his sheep with a dog off the lead. 'Saw a dog up there again this afternoon. Could've been the same one. Completely on her own. No owner in sight. Took a pot shot at her, I did, too. Just to frighten her. Don't think I hit her, but I don't expect to see that one around again . . .' Joe knew all about our little episode with Scrappy up at Black Gill that day. And he knew that George Botham was in fact one of the best shots around.

I interrupted Tom. 'But Black Gill's miles away – it took us ages to drive there when we went.'

'It's not far cross country,' Tom said, 'especially if you wade through the river once or twice. The Rowlinsons took me fishing there and we walked all the way.'

'Anyway, go on. So Joe thought they were talking about Scrappy, did he?'

Joe knew right off that Botham was talking about Scrappy. He also felt sure he'd hit her, otherwise she'd have come home. What really worried him was the fact that Botham didn't shoot to kill. It would have been simpler if he had. So Joe hiked over there and just walked his way round all the fields with sheep in. He followed the stream down to our swimming place, in case Scrappy was looking for us somehow. And that's where he found her, on our little beach. She was a complete mess. Botham's 'pot shot' had caught her shoulder and then she'd cut her leg running away. Joe picked her up and carried her. That's what took him so long. He kept thinking she was going to die before he got her home. He could see the wound, though, so he could tell that the shot hadn't penetrated beyond the bone – which was lucky really.

We were both silent for a bit, just imagining it all. And imagining life without a daffy dog around.

'How's Scrappy now?' I asked.

'Mum said the vet sedated her, so she just looks asleep. The vet's coming again this evening. Were taking it in turns to Scrappy-sit. Ollie doesn't mind. Says he feels they have something in common.'

'Of course! Poor Ollie! How's his ankle? There were so many dramas yesterday I'd completely forgotten about him.'

'Ollie's just fed up. He's OK but he'll be on crutches for a while, so no sport.'

'Not even swimming?' I realised the Water Warriors fixture might be in jeopardy.

'Dunno,' said Tom, bored with the subject of Ollie. 'Are you getting up, or not?'

As nonchalantly as I could, I asked, 'So what are the Rowlinsons up to today? What day is it, anyway?'

'Saturday. They sent Joe to bed at lunchtime. He's been checking on his patient all morning, "past sleeping" he said. Then he conked out over his soup. Kate's downstairs with Ned. And Josh has gone fishing with his dad. Look, are you getting up?'

The coast was clear. 'Yeah, sure,' I said. 'Bog off, then! Can't a girl get some privacy round here?' And Tom dodged his way, laughing, out of the door.

I had a shower and dressed and went downstairs feeling almost human. There was a big notice on the kitchen door saying 'KNOCK FIRST, THEN WAIT' so I did. I heard someone creaking towards the door and realised it was Ollie on his crutches. 'Come in,' he whispered as he opened the door. 'We're trying to keep Scrappy in hospital conditions.' Scrappy had a bed of towels in the corner and she was fenced round with fire guards and airing racks. 'No little ones allowed. You are though.' He creaked back to the kitchen table, which I saw had been well scrubbed since the morning, and looked back at me. 'Very popular you are round here. Can't move for people singing your praises. Charlotte, you're blushing!'

'You know me, Ollie. I blush at anything.'

'First it was Mum – "Charlotte was *so* supportive last night," and then it was Kate – "Charlotte was *really* nice to me last night," and then it was Josh' – here he did another blush-check – ' "Wasn't Charlotte *brilliant* with Kate?" ' I really was blushing now, because I knew he hadn't finished. 'But your greatest admirer, Charlotte, is my hard mate Joe. He kept on about how *excellent* you were with Scrappy and how you *anticipated* his every move. I had to say "Hang on, mate. Don't get ideas above your station. It's your big brother that Cousin Charlotte is gagging for—'''

'Ollie!'

Ollie grinned. 'Sorry, Charl. I just can't see the attraction myself. Josh is such a surly so-and-so.'

'*Ollie!*' I shrieked, and lunged at him. He fended me off with one of his crutches. Scrappy whimpered.

'Now look what you've done!' he laughed as quietly as he could. 'And Charlotte – you've gone very red!' Little did he know why.

I made myself a sandwich and left Ollie, still smirking, to his dog-sitting. I went out into the garden to be with Viv. She was hanging out the washed towels. Ned and Kate were deeply involved in some elaborate game. 'Hi Charlotte. Come and talk to me.' Viv sat down on the grass and gestured for me to join her. 'Tell me everything.'

It was great to go over it all now everyone was safe. Viv was very complimentary about my role in the proceedings. I let her approval wash over me like the sun.

'I do apologise for coming so unhinged last night, Charl. I can cope with most things. I do cope with most things. But that dog – somehow she brings out emotions that I've kept under wraps since Jim's accident – at least, that's the only way I can explain it. I still don't know what I'm going to do about her.'

'Is it too late to get Joe to train her? I know he wants to.'

'Maybe. Perhaps her convalescence will be like a second childhood and she'll be trainable. But I don't know. You know what they say about old dogs and new tricks! Though I'm beginning to think that if anyone could train her, it's Joe. He's got a remarkable way with animals. The vet said that Scrappy should never have survived being carried all that way, let alone kitchen-table surgery. But somehow Joe did exactly the right things. She was very impressed.'

I didn't want to get any deeper into a conversation about Joe at that moment, so I just leant back against the wall and turned my face into the sun.

'We can take it easy this afternoon. There's nothing to do but keep an eye on Scrappy, and that's something Ollie can do. Yesterday was quite enough excitement for an entire summer. We need time to get over it before Joe's birthday bonanza on Wednesday. Maybe Ollie will have recovered enough to swim by then. And maybe Scrappy will be well enough to leave behind!'

Water Warriors was a nice general topic of conversation. I could handle this. 'Who's organising it? We've never actually done Water Warriors on Joe's birthday before, have we? Are we going to have tea and cake and stuff? Will Louise even take time off work?'

'Who knows? I'm happy to organise a birthday picnic. I'm fond of Joe, he's a nice lad. And I owe him one. You'll help, won't you? We could make a cake, buy some crisps. Take ice-cream in the cool bag . . . In fact—' she jumped to her feet, 'why don't we go over to the boathouse now and case the joint? I feel like getting out, trying out the car. Joe's going fishing when he wakes up, so he'll be nicely out of the way. Ollie can stay with the dog, Tom and the little kids can come with us, and we'll be back in a couple of hours. OK?'

'Sounds OK to me.'

The little kids were easily persuaded. The boathouse is on a small private lake. Viv has known the owners for years. No one else uses it, so it's ramshackle and scruffy in the nicest sort of way.

We parked by the roadside and went in through a gate. It's only a short walk through some woods to the lake. The boathouse is about the size of a garage, and stone built. There's a picnic bench in it and, surprisingly, a fireplace. We checked out the wooden dinghy and a fibreglass one, both very basic but still seaworthy. I came across the remains of a raft the boys had tried to construct from logs last year. With a bit of work it might be pressed into service again.

'Let's reckon on good weather, shall we?' said Viv, 'and bring the bench outside. Then the boathouse can be the changing room. We can light the fire – there's luxury!'

'How many will we be?'

'Let's see – you, me and my three, that's five – five

Rowlinsons, that's ten . . . That's plenty actually. Even eight would seem like a party if John and Louise decide not to come. Shame Michelle won't be here. Never mind. She'll be here soon enough.'

'Let's gather some wood now. The kids would be good at that.'

While we were picking up sticks Tom, Ned and Kate discussed the various boats we had at our disposal. Kate said, 'There are two dinghies, but only two paddles, so that has to be one paddle for each dingy. We've got a lilo—'

'And we've got an inflatable dinghy,' said Ned.

'What about the raft?' I asked them. 'I don't remember it being here last year.'

'Joe and Ollie started it last summer,' said Tom, 'but they never managed to finish it somehow. It's cool though. It didn't sink. Perhaps they can use it this year. Now Ollie's such a cripple I reckon we can let them be a pair. You'll still be a middling with me, won't you Charlotte?'

'I'm going with Josh,' said Kate.

'And I'm going with Mum,' said Ned.

'So that leaves my mum and dad to go together,' said Kate. 'And they're both really hopeless!'

Tom and I decided to bag the inflatable dinghy. It didn't have paddles, but it was hard to overturn. Roll on Wednesday!

We had gathered plenty of sticks to pile up by the fireplace. A woodstore lent a homely air to the boathouse. 'It might be fun to brew up if we get a good fire going,' said Viv. 'And if we bring blankets for cold swimmers – no one will ever want to leave!'

On the journey back my stomach lurched at the thought of having to see either Josh or Joe. I tried to marshall my thoughts. Nothing had happened with Joe, after all, nothing as far as he was concerned, anyway. I'd just given a tired boy a hug. That was all. Anyone would have. His mother would have. He was only young. He wouldn't have made anything of it. As for Josh. Well, you never could tell with Josh. Anything for attention, anything for effect. But he had kissed me. Properly. It hadn't just been a peck on the cheek. Or even a peck on the lips, for that matter. It had been the real thing, real tonsil hockey. Aagh. My legs turned to jelly, even there in the car. I mean, could it be that I was his girlfriend now – carrying on where we left off? (Don't be ridiculous Charlotte.) What was I going to say? Should I go up to him and slip a proprietorial arm around his waist? I *don't* think so. No, the more I considered it, the more I thought I should just behave as normal, as if nothing out of the ordinary had happened. After all, Josh played games. Joe didn't. But Josh did.

The kids were making up silly rhymes. 'Ned the bed!' they shrieked. 'Kate the bate!' 'Tom the – Tom the bomb!' 'Mum the bum!' Ned was beside himself with laughter. 'Charlotte the harlot!' That was all I needed. Never mind the fact that Ned didn't have a clue what a harlot was.

*

We got home just before the vet drove up. Ollie was tired and his leg was hurting. Scrappy looked dreadful. I felt rather depressed. Anti-climax I suppose. I had supper with the others and told Viv I was going up for an early night. Tomorrow would be OK as long as I didn't have to face Josh and Joe *together*.

Ten

I felt a lot better when I woke up on Sunday, and ready to face almost anything. All my talking to myself had worked and I decided that, however much I wished it was otherwise, Josh had merely been thanking me in his own way for finding Kate and that nothing the slightest bit significant had happened between me and Joe. That was until I opened the curtains and saw the two brothers standing together in the yard, two tall dark figures, Josh taller and slightly stooped, Joe more upright and solid. Like a coward I drew the curtains again and dived back into bed. I could hear them talking, their voices strangely similar, but I couldn't hear what they were saying. Any moment now, I thought, they are going to come in, together, and then what will I *do*?

But they didn't come in. I waited, expectantly, but noises in our house went on the same as usual and noises in the yard and the Rowlinsons' house stopped altogether. In the end curiosity got the better of me. I dressed and went downstairs. Viv and the boys were having breakfast. Scrappy was in her corner still, but looking slightly better. Everything was completely quiet and normal. The boys grunted at me through their Sugar Puffs. Viv looked up from the Sunday papers and said 'Hi. Help yourself to breakfast, love.'

I looked hard at everyone. Was all this normality fake? No. It was genuine. The drama was over everywhere apart from in my head. Soon Ollie was hobbling around complaining about his sore ankle. Ned was playing on Tom's Gameboy. Tom wasn't complaining – he wanted me to do things with him. Viv was clearing up. Nobody seemed the slightest bit bothered or interested in what the Rowlinsons were doing.

And so it went on all day. I phoned Mum and Dad. They said they'd heard from Michelle and that she was having a fantastic time and had a terrific tan. Mum said she'd seen some of my friends around and that they'd asked after me. There was a card from Maddy. It all seemed so far removed from life up here. I tried ringing Hannah, but her dad said she was still away. Pity. I would have appreciated Hannah's opinions on my present situation.

I gathered that the Rowlinsons were all out for the

day – they didn't often get the chance to do things as a family. But I didn't dare ask any more. No one mentioned them, let alone in connection with me. It struck me that of course they just didn't *know*. No one had seen me with Josh or even considered that anything might be going on. They all knew I'd fancied him for ever. Dumpy old Charlotte being in love with Josh was just part of the holiday fortnight. And as for Joe – something happening between the two of us would never have occurred to anyone, least of all me. I caught myself blushing at that moment. I blushed deeper when Viv appeared to read my thoughts and asked the boys if they had any ideas about Joe's birthday, and did any of them want to go shopping with her on Tuesday. Then she asked me what I was like at cake-making because she was lousy. Did I feel up to making a cake for Joe? Should it be a chocolate cake?

And so it went on. A nice calm day. That night, as I was walking back into the kitchen after hanging up some washing, someone waved to me from the Rowlinsons' window. I waved back. I never saw who it was.

On Monday morning Tom and I were helping Viv in the kitchen when my worst nightmare came true. Josh and Joe came in *together*. Joe smiled at me briefly from under his fringe and quickly asked Viv where Ollie was. He wanted to show him something up by the weir and could he get there on crutches?

As Viv was answering him Josh came up to me, held out his arms in a theatrical way and said, 'Charlotte. Gissa a kiss. I've missed you.' He proceeded to wrap his arms around me and kiss me fulsomely on the lips. 'Lovely girl. Viv, I'm going to take her away from all this. All work and no play makes Charlotte a dull girl!' I was too flabbergasted to interject, but I caught a glimpse of Joe disappearing in search of Ollie, and of Tom's disgusted face before he followed Joe.

Viv appeared to take this new development in her stride and, scarcely batting an eyelid, said, 'Of course. Go and enjoy yourself, Cinderella. See you at lunchtime!'

Josh grabbed my hand and led me off down towards the river. It sounds romantic, but actually I wanted to go to the loo and if I had been expecting a romantic encounter I would have shaved my legs. And I certainly wouldn't have worn jeans that didn't do up properly because they were too tight round the waist. So I followed slightly reluctantly. But Josh was sprightly, full of the joys of spring. He practically danced down the path. To be honest, I was so shocked by this turn of events that I just followed him.

He led me to a sheltered corner of the field that ran alongside the river – in the opposite direction from the weir, I was glad to see. It was a warm, sunny spot, well hidden from the path. Well hidden from anything, in fact. I tried not to panic. Josh took off his jacket and laid it on the grass. He sat down on it and patted a place next to him. When I hesitated he reached up and grabbed my hand and pulled me down beside him. I sat rather stiffly, but he put his arm around me and bent his head to kiss me again, skilfully (I realised) lying me on my back as he did so. He carried on kissing me and leant the whole weight of his chest on mine – no way could I escape.

I thought I was doing OK, but next time he drew breath he whispered, 'Relax, Charlotte, relax. I'm not going to hurt you. Move your arms. Put them round my neck.' I realised that I'd been holding my hands together protectively over my chest. It hadn't been very comfortable, but with Josh's weight I hadn't been able to move them. Gingerly I put my arms around his neck. We were so close, it was scary. Here I was lying in a field with the boy of my dreams. His face was pressing on mine and he was kissing me. I had my arms around his neck and I was running my hands through his hair. He had his hands . . . Hang on, he had his hands pushing up under my T-shirt, and I wasn't sure that I wanted him to. This wasn't simply prudishness (I tried to tell myself) – I was worried he might grab my spare tyre by mistake. I'd had groping sessions with boys at parties before now, and they usually took slightly longer to get to this stage. And I wanted to enjoy the kissing bit for the moment. What's more, I still wanted to go to the loo and I was more than ever aware of my stubbly legs and . . . Dammit, *I didn't want this right now*! I hadn't had any say in the matter.

'Josh. Please. No,' I said, and tried to sit up.

'What's the matter?' he mumbled, and tried to push me down again.

'Josh – I – I – *I want to go to the toilet*!'

The spell was broken. Josh moved off me and sat up. But as he did, I was aware of two familiar figures crossing the end of the field at a point where they could have seen us. One of them was on crutches. Oh my God. They disappeared from my view as I took in Josh's outraged face. 'What's the matter with you, Charlotte?'

'Josh—' I felt rather weepy – 'Josh, I just don't feel quite ready, for . . . for all this.'

'For God's sake, Charlotte. I'm not going to rape you. Just a bit of fooling around. Don't you like fooling around?'

I did, but I didn't know how to say so without him pouncing on me again, and I was still desperate for the loo.

'Josh. I know this isn't very romantic, but I'm going into the bushes over there for a pee. And then I'll come back and then I'll talk sensibly. OK?' Josh grunted and I dived self-consciously into the farthest, thickest bushes I could find. When I returned, he was looking thoughtful.

'Charl, I thought this was what you wanted. I – All the others are always telling me how you – and I feel—'

This wasn't getting anywhere. 'It is, Josh. It is what I wanted. But I'm four years younger than you and I'm inexperienced and well – I'm just a bit scared of you. I never know what you really think.' I looked at him. It was the closest thing to an honest conversation we'd ever had. He stayed sitting on the grass. He smoothed his trousers down and wouldn't look at me. I saw the cynical Josh kick in.

'Run along home, little girl,' he said, narrowing his eyes. 'The old man *vants to be alone*,' and he lay on his jacket with his back to me.

I made my way back to the house, praying that I wouldn't bump into anyone. Viv was in the kitchen. She looked at my rumpled clothes but didn't refer to them. 'Lunch in half an hour,' she said, 'you can shell these peas.' I sat down at the kitchen table with them. I couldn't think of a thing to say. Viv hummed to herself and carefully didn't ask me anything. The door opened. Joe put his head round, took one look at me and hastily withdrew. Scrappy heaved a doggy sigh.

Tom came in. 'Don't like real peas,' he complained and also went out again.

Ollie creaked in, winked at me salaciously and sat down. He spoke to Viv. 'Me and Joe want to go and work on the raft this afternoon, Mum. Will you take us over to the boathouse? I can work on it sitting down, but I'm getting around quite well now. Aren't I Charl?'

I carried on furiously podding peas.

'We could take Tom. Though he's in a foul mood at the moment. Dunno why. But we might cheer him up. You won't want to be coming with us *younger* boys, now, will you, Charl?'

I said nothing. I couldn't bear the thought that Joe must have seen me with Josh. Just when I'd been trying to push him off me. How must it have looked? 'I'm not feeling too good, Viv,' I said. 'In fact I feel a bit sick.' (I did.) 'I'm going to go and lie down. Don't worry about lunch for me,' and I ran upstairs to hide in my room. I knew I was hiding, and I wasn't proud of myself. It was just that Josh's behaviour first thing this morning had been so unexpected. There was me telling myself that him kissing me in the yard had all been a horrible mistake and then he'd done completely the opposite to what I'd forecast. Then all that snogging business in the field. I wasn't ready. I wasn't prepared. Had I really been a complete wet? Some of it had been quite nice. What could Josh think of me? Josh, Josh. The love of my life. Perhaps I could try again. I do like fooling around, though I prefer it in the dark. Aagh. I just didn't know.

Viv called upstairs to say that she was taking the boys off to the boathouse, that Ned was next door with Kate and could I let the vet in when she called round later on. I lay in bed reading to take my mind off things. I was reading *Pride and Prejudice*, lovely

Jane Austen (I've seen nearly all of them on video), all romantic where no one even so much as kisses. How much simpler life must have been in those days. There was a ring at the doorbell.

I thought it must be the vet, but it wasn't, it was Josh. At the front door. He looked embarrassed.

'Josh! Why have you come to the front door?'

'Because I knew you wouldn't answer the back door.'

'What do you want?' Somehow he had wrong-footed me all over again.

'I want you to come to the cinema with me tonight.'

'What?' Oops. That sounded rather rude. I said it more politely. 'What?'

'There's a film I want to see, and it would be more fun to go with someone. And I want to apologise for jumping you this morning.'

I looked at him with my mouth open. 'What?' I said again.

'Charlotte, don't make me say all that again. Please, pretty please, will you come out to the cinema with me tonight, for pity's sake!'

'You mean, go *out* with you?'

'Yes, Charlotte, go out to the cinema with me.'

I supposed that would be all right. 'All right,' I said.

'Good,' he said. 'That's settled then. I'll wait in my car down on the road at eight. OK?'

'OK,' I said. He squeezed my hands quickly and

went away, leaving me standing, still gawping, on the front doorstep to face the vet.

Scrappy was on the mend. This was good because it meant that she wasn't going to die. But it was bad because it meant she was getting some of her energy back and couldn't be penned up all the time. It meant we had to start worrying about her getting into trouble again. I asked the vet if she thought we might be able to retrain her.

'It's worth a try,' she said. 'And if anyone can do it, your lad next door probably can. I can't believe he's only fifteen – he acted as well as any adult over this business.'

'He's fourteen,' I said. 'Nearly fourteen.'

I left the others having supper when I heard Josh tooting in the lane. Tom was still in a bad mood, which was very unlike him.

'I'm going out to the cinema,' I said. 'I'll be back about eleven,' and scarpered. As I went out I could hear Tom saying 'It's not *fair*! Charlotte was going to play with *me* tonight. And we were going to start planning our Warriors tactics . . .'

I got into the car and Josh leaned over to give me a kiss. (Blimey, I thought, this is like a real couple already.) 'Let's go,' he said. 'We must leave some time to park.'

The film was a 15. There wasn't a problem about me getting in. But there was quite a lot of sex in it.

And it's one thing giggling with my friends in Sophie's loft, but quite another watching it with Josh. He had his hand on my thigh, and squeezed rather tightly when things got steamy. And he was very keen on snogging in the boring bits, which meant I lost track of the plot and the people behind us started to mutter. I was still having to work to convince myself that this was what I wanted. It was just so strange after all these years of hero-worship-ping Josh. Now I 'had' him it didn't seem quite right. And to make things more complicated, Josh took me straight home afterwards, kissed me on the cheek and left me on the doorstep.

I went in. Viv had gone to bed. Ollie and Joe were watching television. They had Scrappy up on the sofa with them and Joe was stroking her. I said 'Hi.' Ollie grinned at me and waved one of his crutches. Joe attempted a smile – and failed. He got up suddenly and Scrappy landed awkwardly. Joe patted her and shot off home, leaving me to help Scrappy into the kitchen and Ollie up the stairs.

Eleven

I woke up early on Tuesday morning. I was glad because it gave me time to think – and boy, did I need to think. What hit me first was that although I should have been delirious with happiness, I wasn't.

The main problem, quite apart from my mixed-up emotions, was the way my altered relationship with Josh upset the balance of my relationships with everyone else. Perhaps that's what happens when you grow up. I was overcome with that terrible scary feeling you get when you think that nothing will ever be the same again. It was one thing me fancying Josh and the boys all teasing me about it, but quite another when I went from their junior camp into his senior one. I had suddenly become a Girl – with a capital letter – overnight. I should have been glad that it forced them to look at me differently, but I wasn't, especially as I still felt like the same old Charlotte. Perhaps it was wrong that Ollie liked to tease me about Josh. Perhaps it was wrong that Ned and Tom loved me unconditionally like a big sister. Perhaps it was wrong that part of Josh's role was to be horrible to me and make me blush. But it had always been like that. Before. And now it wasn't.

I tried to analyse my feelings for Josh. He was gorgeous, he was sexy – but he was no longer unattainable. He was still enigmatic, he still frightened me, but he seemed to *want* to be with me. I couldn't understand why. I was only me, Charlotte. I had a sneaky suspicion, which I tried to quell, that it was because I was the only Girl around. After all, last year Josh had fancied my sister.

I was so confused, and there was no one I could talk to about it. I reminded myself firmly that I was totally in love with Josh and always had been, but I must admit, I wasn't altogether convinced.

Meanwhile, it was Joe's birthday tomorrow and there were presents to buy, a party to prepare and a cake to bake. Tom needed my attention – he'd missed out lately – and we did need to plan our Water Warriors tactics. And I needed to think about Michelle arriving and what we would all want to do once she was here. If only I could put the whole Josh thing on hold. I hoped he wasn't going to be too demanding.

I went down to breakfast. The first thing I noticed was an absence of dog. 'Where's Scrappy?' I asked, shocked.

Viv answered. 'When I came down this morning she was all floppy and panting, trying to move but not able to. So I called the vet. She was here about an hour ago. She was worried about Scrappy's leg rather than the shot wound and thought that she'd better X-ray it so she's taken her to the surgery. She's got her under observation today and if necessary she'll operate tomorrow. I feel guilty, but it's a relief not having a dog underfoot right now.'

I thought Tom was going to add something at that point, but it became obvious that Tom simply wasn't talking to me. Ned was off with Kate some-where and while I ate my toast Ollie and Viv were deep in discussion about Joe's birthday. Viv turned to me. 'Do you still want to make Joe's cake?' she asked me.

'Why ever not?' I retorted rather too quickly.

'I just thought you might have other things to do today,' she said vaguely.

'Like snogging with Joe's brother,' said Ollie under his breath.

'Of course I'll do Joe's cake,' I said, trying to ignore everything that they were implying. 'What sort do you think he'll want, Ollie? Chocolate?'

Just then Josh came in, with Joe trailing behind. Josh came up behind me and put his arms round my waist. 'Well, what's on the agenda for us today, pretty girl?'

Tom made puking noises and dashed out of the kitchen. Ollie caught Joe's eye and, when he thought I couldn't see him, pointed his fingers down his throat. I pulled away from Josh. 'We're organising tomorrow and I'm making the birthday cake. What sort do you want Joe?' I said to the shadowy figure hanging around outside the kitchen door.

'Oi, Joe, come in here when the lady's talking to you,' called Josh. Joe came in past Ollie, who muttered, 'That's no lady . . .'

'You really don't have to make me a cake, Charlotte,' said Joe, looking at his feet and shuffling like a small boy. 'I don't usually have one.'

'Yeah. Surely we've all got better things to do,' leered Josh.

This was awful. 'I've said I'll make a cake, OK?' I said. 'Joe—' I forced him to look me in the eye – 'I want to make you a birthday cake. Now what sort do you want?'

Joe flashed me one of his intense looks before glancing down again, his cheeks flushed, and answering, 'Thanks. Chocolate.'

Josh jeered. 'Chocky cake for diddums, then, Charlotte. Smarties on it Joe? Do you want it in any particular shape, little bro?' He turned to me. 'So when do you spare a lecherous old man some of your time?'

Ollie swung past us to the door and went out with Joe. I didn't know where. Viv, who'd been loading the dishwasher with her back to me up until now looked round, an eyebrow raised. I felt wretched. Josh was doing this all wrong.

'Well, I'm going to the supermarket quite soon,' said Viv. 'I can buy the ingredients, or you can come with me and choose them yourself.'

'You buy them Viv,' said Josh, before I could answer.

'And we've still got some organising to do,' Viv continued.

'I really don't see why you're making such a fuss about Joe's birthday,' said Josh, beginning to sound petulant. I could see that Viv was fed up with him, but it was me she spoke to. I could hear the irritation in her voice.

'I don't mind what you do this morning, Charl,

but I'm going to need you here this afternoon when I take Ollie to the hospital for a check-up. And we must set aside a couple of hours for tomorrow's preparation. It's up to you of course. Just let me know before I go in half an hour what your plans are.'

I wanted Josh to go away and give me time to sort myself out. I wished he wouldn't come over so early. It had disrupted yesterday and it looked like disrupting today as well. I found myself feeling guilty for not wanting to be with him. I said to him as tactfully as I could, 'Josh could you just give me a few minutes to sort myself out?'

'In other words, "Bog off, Josh." OK, but I'll be back in half an hour too.'

Viv watched as Josh left, but she didn't say anything. What on earth was happening! I even felt awkward with Viv now. Then she spoke. 'I won't interfere, Charlotte. But just don't let the boys – any of them, not even the younger ones – put pressure on you. OK? Take your time, is my advice. See you in a bit!' And I was left in the kitchen on my own.

The kettle was hot, so I made myself some coffee. There was a notepad and pencil on the table where Viv had been making a shopping list. I turned to a fresh page and picked up the pencil. I divided the page into six, the number of days left of the holiday. It seemed extraordinary that the end was already in sight, even though so much had happened. Today was Tuesday. Tomorrow, Wednesday, was the Water Warriors party. Thursday was blank. And on Friday evening, Michelle arrived! I wondered what on earth Michelle would make of Josh and me as an item! I couldn't see it somehow. I forced myself to think about the day ahead. Maybe Viv could buy the cake things and I could spend some time with Josh. Why not, it was what I wanted, wasn't it? Well, wasn't it? I wondered what Josh had in mind.

I went and shaved my legs and spent quite a while in the loo.

'So what's the plan?' asked Viv when I went down.

'Can you get cocoa and cooking chocolate and fondant icing for me? I want to make a cake like Joe and Ollie's raft, Viv. What do you think would be best? Chocolate flakes? No –Twixes. Can you get me about £3 worth? I'll pay you back. And some of that icing you can write with. And some candles.' I wanted Joe's cake to be good.

'Fine,' said Viv. 'What about a present?'

'I just can't decide what he'd like. Joe's someone you feel you have to get exactly the right present for, isn't he?'

Viv laughed. 'I shouldn't try too hard. I'm sure this amazing cake will be good enough.' Ollie hobbled in. 'What do you think would be a good present for Joe from Charlotte, Ol?' For reply, Ollie gave a disgusting laugh.

Viv raised her eyes to heaven. 'See you later, Charl.'

Josh called for me and we set off for a walk. He didn't hold my hand or put his arm round my shoulder – we walked separately, he determinedly and me tagging along after him. I thought maybe he was annoyed with me. Why could I never tell what he was thinking?

'Is everything all right?' I asked.

'Yes. Why shouldn't it be?'

'You just seem – a bit—'

'A bit what?'

'A bit, well, in a hurry.'

I saw where Josh was heading. There was an old barn where hay used to be stored. We'd played there a lot one year as kids. It seemed as if more fooling around was about to take place. It seemed as if Josh was calling all the shots.

Josh reached for my hand and led me inside the rickety barn door. There were holes above the rafters where birds hopped about and a little light filtered in, but otherwise it was dim, like a church. He shut the door and leant against it, pulling me to him. I leant my head against his chest. It felt comfortable and I would have liked to stay like that for a while, but soon he was pushing my face up with his to kiss me. He held me very tightly, too tightly, and ran his hands up and down my back, up and down, fever-ishly. Like a four-legged creature he tried to steer us towards the bales of hay. I was shuffling along backwards and it would have been funny if it hadn't all felt so urgent. We literally fell onto the hay bales. I wanted Josh to talk to me, but he was breathing heavily and starting to fumble with the buttons on my blouse. 'Josh – please, let me talk . . .'

'Oh no, here we go again. Talk, talk. Charlotte, you're supposed to be enjoying yourself. You are here, in a wonderful hay barn with me, the cool, fit bloke of your dreams, remember?'

'I know. I'm sorry, Josh. I just – it just – doesn't feel right. I know I've been in love with you for ages, but I don't – I'm not sure that I really *love* you.'

'I don't believe this! What's love got to do with it? What's love, if it comes to that? I *fancy* you Charlotte. You've grown up and I fancy you. Doesn't that mean anything to you?'

I looked at him. No. I could hardly believe the stark truth myself, but after an eternity of longing for Josh to notice me, fancy me, it didn't really mean anything. I thought it would have done, but right now it didn't. I was alone with Josh in a hay barn – and I wanted to be a million miles away. I wanted him to *love* me, but I didn't know how to tell him. So I let him persuade me to lie down, and I let him have a certain amount of his wicked way with me. And I hated myself.

Josh looked at his watch. 'Hey! Home time!' he said cheerfully. I stood up. I was covered in hay.

'Brush yourself down, gorgeous. We don't want everyone knowing where we've been.' I smiled weakly.

Josh was trying to be nice, I realised. And I also realised that I didn't really like him any more. I felt gutted.

We went in at our separate doors. Viv was on the point of setting off to the hospital with Ollie. 'I've put all the cake stuff out,' she said. 'The little ones are full of plans for tomorrow – I hope it's not all too frenetic for you. Bye! See you later.'

'Charlotte! Can we help you make the cake? Please?' said Kate.

'Can I lick the bowl?' begged Ned.

Tom sat and scowled.

'I want to make some drawings before I begin,' I told them. 'It's going to be a raft like the one Joe and Ollie have built. But I haven't worked it out exactly yet and I need to do that first.'

I sat down at the kitchen table with Ned and Kate on either side of me. Tom sat at the far end. He wasn't talking yet, but at least he was still there. I tried to catch his eye and smile at him. I wanted to say, Don't be jealous Tom. I love you just the same. This is another bit of Charlotte that you don't know and don't need to know. And anyway, right now, I don't think there's much to be jealous of. But I didn't say it of course, and if I had, Josh's appearance almost immediately would have seemed very odd. Josh squeezed in between me and Kate, an arm round each of us. Kate didn't like it. She decided to test him out.

'Josh, you haven't forgotten that you're my partner in Water Warriors tomorrow, have you?'

Josh has never taken Water Warriors as seriously as the others, and he had in fact forgotten his promise to Kate. He chose this moment, the wrong moment, to be flippant. 'Don't you think I ought to be my girlfriend's partner, Kate?'

Kate's eyes blazed and she beat Josh on the chest with her fists. 'But Josh, you promised! You *promised* you'd be my partner. And we're a big and a little. You couldn't possibly go with Charlotte because then you'd be two bigs and that wouldn't be fair. And anyway, who would I go with then?'

Josh tried to fend off the rain of blows, but Kate was beside herself. She was crying now. 'It's not fair, it's not fair. Why do you have to go and spoil everything?' and ran out of the room.

Suddenly Tom was beside me, white-faced and angry. 'It's Charlotte who's spoiled everything. We were all right before you came, Charlotte. Even Scrappy was all right before you came. And though you might not remember, you were going to be *my* partner tomorrow. But I don't want to be your partner now, not ever. In fact I hate you. I hate Josh and I hate you even more.' Tom's voice cracked. 'And you've upset Kate, so she'll probably run away again and it'll be all your fault. Come on

99

Ned, let's not stay here. Let's go and play next door.'
And they left too.

'I'd better go after Kate,' said Josh. 'Well, the apple
cart has been well and truly upset. I'll see you later.'

I was on my own in the kitchen again. Tom's
outburst had been the last straw. Dear, loyal Tom,
my champion. What had I done?

I started on the chocolate cakes, good, mindless
work, that helped me forget the mess I was in. I
shoved the tins of chocolate mixture in the oven
and began moulding two little figures of Joe and
Ollie to go on the raft. I coloured some of the icing
as near to flesh colour as I could get. It looked pink –
a good match for Ollie, but not for Joe. I thought
about the lovely golden tan colour of his skin. I
added a drop of green and a drop of yellow to the
pink. It was getting there. Then I did some red and
some black for their swimming shorts before playing with the colours for their hair. I used yellow
with a little brown for Ollie, and then brown for Joe.
I added the yellow to Joe's in fine streaks, just like
the gloss on his hair when the sun shone on it.

I sat back. The cakes were beginning to smell
good. I looked at my handiwork and felt really
pleased with it. And then I remembered what had
gone before.

I thought of the way everything had gone so
wrong. Everyone was so upset, and all for nothing. I
didn't love Josh. It was unbelievable, but I didn't.
Nor did I want the others to think I did. The

awfulness of it all washed over me. I could feel the lump in my throat and my eyes brimming. The cakes were ready. I got them out and put them on racks and then sat down again. The tears were coming down so fast I couldn't see any more. I laid my head on my arms and cried my heart out.

I didn't hear the tap on the door or see Joe coming in. I wasn't aware of anything until I felt a tissue being pushed at me. I looked up into Joe's concerned face.

'Here, have another tissue. You look hideous.'

'Thanks a bunch.'

'Good, I made you smile.'

Joe pulled up a chair. He looked at what I'd been making.

'You weren't supposed to see that until tomorrow.'

He picked up the little Joe figure. 'Is this me?' He laughed incredulously and put it down.

I sniffed. 'Where are the others?'

'All out.'

I relaxed slightly.

'What's the matter, Charlotte? You can talk to me if you want.'

I grinned wanly. 'That doesn't really seem fair.'

'I'm not blind, Charl, and I do know my brother. I know how difficult he finds it to be consistent with people. I love him too, you know, but he's still a weirdo. Now, tell me about it. Talk to Uncle Joe.'

Who was this amazingly mature person? He was being so sweet, I just started to cry all over again.

'Try,' he said. 'You've got half an hour before anyone comes back. I know, I checked.'

'Well,' I began. And then I found myself telling him everything. Well, almost everything. There were some details I omitted, but somehow I managed to say that I was no longer in love with his brother. I told him how worried I was that everyone hated me and that holidays here would never be the same again. Then he stopped me. He held my shoulders.

'Charlotte, no one *hates* you – it's because they all *love* you that this has happened. Don't you see?' He gave me his intense Joe gaze. (Why is it that boys always seem to be blessed with the longest, darkest lashes?) 'But you must talk to Josh and put him straight. I don't approve of girls who lead guys on,' he said sanctimoniously. 'In his funny old way, Josh must be fond of you and he also has his pride, misplaced though it is sometimes. You must be careful not to hurt his pride.'

I heard a car approaching. 'Promise me you'll talk to him tonight,' said Joe. 'I don't like seeing you so miserable.' He touched my cheek as he left. I felt as if I'd been scorched.

Twelve

I went back to making the cake. Gradually, the others drifted in. The younger ones had been watching television next door, which was why Joe was able to predict how long they'd be. Josh had gone into town to get a birthday present. The mood had changed. Obviously Josh had mollified Kate a little and Ned wasn't taking sides. Tom came in behind Ollie and Viv. The cake was more or less finished, and I have to say it did look good.

'Wow!' said Ollie as he came in. 'That looks good enough to eat! Look at this Tom. Cousin Charlotte is good on the pie front isn't she?'

'The cake's OK,' said Tom guardedly.

'I've still got to add the writing and the candles, but then it's finished. Can we work out our tactics after supper, Tom?' I asked.

He looked at me. 'Maybe,' was all he would say. But somehow I thought he might come round.

Because I was already in cooking mode I offered to get supper. I made a lasagne, which was everybody's favourite. Isn't it funny how the right food can put everybody in a better mood (especially guys, it seems)? I felt more in control now. Joe had given me the courage to do what I knew was right. So while the lasagne was in the oven I went and knocked next door. Louise let me in. 'I've come to see Josh,' I said, feeling braver than I felt, and hoping that neither Joe nor Kate would suddenly appear. Louise called Josh. 'Hi, Josh,' I said when he came downstairs, and before he could say anything – 'Could we go to the pub later, about half nine?'

Josh didn't want to talk in front of Louise. 'Fine,' he said. 'I'll meet you in the lane at nine-fifteen.'

'OK, see you then,' I said and left quickly, with Louise's words 'Isn't she a bit young for the pub?' just audible. And anyway, I'm not, I thought.

Supper with Viv and the boys was such a cheerful affair that my faith in human nature was restored, even though I was horribly apprehensive about the forthcoming encounter with Josh. Tom saw that I really hadn't changed as much as he'd feared. Afterwards he came and sat by me. Without looking at me he linked his little finger in mine and said, 'Friends again?'

'Of course,' I said. 'Come on Tom, let's go up to your room and make our plans. You know I've bagged the inflatable dinghy for us, don't you?'

'That means we're slow, but hard to tip up,' said Tom. 'OK, I've got some paper and something to write with. Let's go.'

By nine o'clock Tom and I had our strategy all worked out and we were good friends again. I noticed that he wasn't as cuddly as usual, but I suppose that figured – he's always been so tuned in to my feelings. I said goodnight to him and went downstairs.

I told Viv I was going to the pub with Josh, and I told her not to worry. This drink was all about me going at my own pace. 'Well, good luck,' said Viv as I slipped out of the door. I needed it.

I got into the car with Josh. He leant over and kissed me affectionately. He'd washed his hair and he smelt of aftershave. This was going to be difficult. But I had made my promise to Joe. 'Don't hurt Josh's pride,' I reminded myself over and over. The pub was long and low with a log fire, even in summer. Josh bought me my usual Coke and a soft drink for himself. He was very conscientious about not drinking and driving.

We sat down by the fire with our drinks. 'All right, then Charlotte,' he said. 'What's this all about?' He was tapping his foot nervously. 'Come on. You haven't brought me here just to be sociable.'

I had my opening. 'Josh, will you just hear me out before you say anything?'

'I won't promise, but I'll try.'

(Don't hurt his pride. Don't hurt his pride.) 'Ever since I can remember, you've been my hero.'

'—Got a bit sullied, have I?'

'Josh, please. You said you'd listen.' I had to keep going. 'And I got used to having you as my hero, whatever you said to me or did. It was easy really, because hero-worship is sort of two-dimensional –

you never have to examine your real feelings about someone, or their real feelings about you, for that matter. You were just this distant, unattainable guy.'

'So you don't like what you see close up?'

'Josh, shut up. I didn't say that. On this holiday I've got to know you so much better—'

'—I'll say!'

'Josh! I never even knew about your family before. I hadn't noticed how brilliant you were with Kate. I didn't know you had a gentle side. And then, just as I was getting to know these things, we—'

Josh gave me a lopsided grin. 'We what?'

'Well, suddenly we were having a relationship. And it was all too fast – and—' I grabbed his hand and took a deep breath. 'Josh, I don't want us to carry on.'

Josh pulled his hand away. 'Why on earth not? What's the matter with me?'

(Don't hurt his pride.) 'Nothing's the matter with you. It's me. I can't handle it. I'm new to relationships, especially with grown-up blokes like you. It might be different if I could concentrate on it, but I can't because of all the other distractions here. Perhaps if it was just you and me, in a different situation. No little cousins. No injured dogs. No aunts.'

Josh regarded me quizzically. 'You're a serious little thing, aren't you?'

'So? There's nothing wrong with that is there?'

'No, no. And in fact when you were so good about finding Kate, I felt seriously grateful to you. No, more than that. I wanted to let you know how much I liked you for it. And then, well, there you were. A girl. On the spot. I liked you and I thought we could have some fun in this godforsaken place. I thought you'd enjoy it too. Michelle did.'

'*What?*'

'Yeah. Michelle and I enjoyed a little bit of, er – hanky-panky last year. It didn't seem to involve everybody else like it has with you.'

'You had a thing going with my sister last year?' I was incredulous. Michelle was a sneaky cow. We all just thought that Josh fancied her.

'It was nothing, Charl. Just a bit of fun, like I said.'

I was speechless. My thoughts were in a complete whirl. So was Josh more serious about me than about Michelle or was he still just playing games? Honestly, the more I got to know this guy, the more I wished I didn't. And yet his admission seemed to offer a way out.

'Look Josh. You may pretend that you don't have feelings, but you don't fool me. I can't work out what you think about me, about us. But I do care about you, as a person rather than as a hero, and I don't want to hurt your feelings. I just don't want our relationship to go any further and mess up the other things that are important to me. Perhaps, since Michelle's coming, it would be better to stop anyway.'

Josh looked at his watch and got up to go. He held out his hand to me. 'OK. Come on then. Whatever you want.'

We went out to the car. It was a clear night with a sky full of stars. We stood looking up at them for a few minutes. Josh held my hand, his fingers entwined with mine. Then he hugged me in his usual tight Josh-ish way, before pushing me away slightly and resting his arms over my shoulders. He looked down at me and smiled. 'Pity,' he said ruefully, brushing my hair off my face with a sigh, 'you're a lovely squeeze,' and gave me a final, lingering, tender kiss. I could feel my knees buckling and my resolve weakening. But it was too late. My holiday romance was over almost before it had begun. Maybe, when it came to reporting back to the others, I'd pretend it had never happened at all. I'd have to think about that.

'When did you say Michelle was coming?' Josh asked.

Thirteen

I woke up on the morning of Joe's birthday feeling brilliant. I was free again, free of Josh, and it hadn't been too traumatic. I didn't relish seeing him later on, but I felt I could handle it. Now I could enjoy the boathouse bonanza and the rest of the holiday. Even the weather was great.

Joe burst into our kitchen, very much the birth-day boy, to claim his presents. Viv had found a cheap CD-ROM on fishing for him and the boys had bought him a water gun. Of course they had to try it out immediately. Everyone was wet before Viv shooed us out of the kitchen into the yard. While Ollie was dousing his younger brothers I apologised to Joe for not having a present for him. 'Let me know what you want, Joe, and I'll get it for you tomorrow.'

'Seeing you happy again is quite a good present,' he said lightly, his attention on his new toy. He took his eyes off the water fight for a brief moment and flashed me a grin, adding – 'Don't worry, I'm sure I'll think of a better one before the end of today.'

The cars were packed with swimming gear, the lilo, the inflatable dinghy, an enormous picnic, crock-ery, cutlery, Thermoses, water carriers, rugs, folding chairs and over-excited children. Josh took Joe and Ollie, who were every bit as hysterical as the younger ones. We had Ned, Kate and Tom in the back. I sat in the front with the cake on my lap. John and Louise had even agreed to take the afternoon off work and were joining us after lunch.

We parked the cars by the gate and started

carrying everything to the boathouse, quite a laborious business. Josh fell in with me as I carted a hamper down the path and he struggled with the lilo. 'OK?' he asked. I nodded. 'Me too,' he said. It was as if the last barrier to a terrific day had been lifted.

We set up the picnic bench. Tea was going to be the main meal, but Viv had brought pasties for lunch which we ate while making the preparations for the game. The inflatable dinghy needed blowing up and the other dinghies needed cleaning – I was doing that with Viv and Tom. Joe and Ollie – Ollie hopping about without his crutches – were putting the final touches to their raft. Josh was lighting the fire in the boathouse with the little ones looking on. He detailed them to pick up twigs for kindling – I was impressed by the way he managed to occupy them. He also kept them in order by having incredibly strict rules about the fire. Maybe I could like this guy again! But Josh with Kate, I reminded myself, was Josh at his best.

By the time the Rowlinson parents came on the scene, the various craft were lined up on the bank, tea was set, the fire in the boathouse was lit and we were all kitted out in our swimsuits and old trainers. It was actually a hot afternoon. John and Louise, determined to be good sports on this occasion, retired to the boathouse to change and soon joined us. It was amusing to see everyone lined up like that. I even couldn't help noticing that Josh looked rather white and puny compared with the others.

Joe, as VIP for the day, was given the job of blowing the starting whistle. We all got into our boats. Viv and Ned had the old wooden dinghy – and one paddle. The Rowlinsons had the fibreglass dinghy, also with one paddle. Josh and Kate were lying on their fronts across the lilo – you can't sink the lilo but they didn't look too stable. Kate looked very happy snuggling up to her big brother though, and you never knew what tricks Josh might pull out of the bag. He was an ace tipper. Tom and I had the inflatable dinghy – nice and comfortable, but no paddles. We had found a long stick to punt with, and we also paddled with our hands. Joe and Ollie looked very smug on their new raft, but it did have a tendency to spin around. They had also made themselves a punting pole.

We all paddled around for a bit. I saw Josh manoeuvre the lilo some distance from the bank, where it was too deep to wade. He said something to Kate and then slipped overboard and swam underwater towards the raft. I watched as he suddenly shot up and tipped the whole thing over. I was so busy watching that I didn't notice Viv and Ned coming up behind us, Viv paddling very efficiently. Ned leant over and pressed the side of our dinghy down so that it started to fill with water before they paddled off again. Meanwhile, Tom was urging me to head for the Rowlinsons, who, despite having a decent boat and a paddle, had barely left the bank.

Joe and Ollie quickly righted their raft. Joe had his water gun which he squirted at Kate and Josh as Ollie paddled them into the fray. The battle was well under way.

'Come on, Charl, let's get Mum and Ned. I'm going to board their boat and steal their paddle.'

'All's fair in love and war,' I told him, and we headed towards the wooden dinghy.

Josh and Kate now turned their attentions to the Rowlinsons. They floated innocently towards them in their dinghy, which was still in shallow water. Josh wedged the lilo in some reeds and he and Kate both climbed out. Kate swims like a fish, so they made their way underwater to the side of the boat, then both stood up and leant on the side, tipping John and Louise spectacularly into the water. Louise shrieked a bit and then climbed out on to the bank. She was out of the game. John had to let Kate and Josh have his boat and made for the lilo on his own.

Tom carried out the move that we had planned the night before, stealing Viv and Ned's paddle almost before they knew what had hit them. Ned leant out of the dinghy to splash Tom's departing figure and tumbled overboard. He decided that he might be better off with Joe and Ollie and made for their raft.

And so it went on. Our winning manouevre many small battles later was all thanks to Tom. Army general in the making, that one. We swam under-water towards Joe and Ollie's raft. Josh with Kate on his back was also swimming quite slowly towards it. It was easy to see which side they were going to board and follow them below the surface. So as Kate climbed onto the raft – bravely, despite having a water gun trained on her, and as Josh tried to ease himself on board too, Tom and I were ready to pull the raft under from the same side. It worked a dream. The raft overturned and we had all five of them in the water – just like that!

The real battle was over, and Tom and I had definitely won, no one disputed it, but we all splashed around for a bit until Viv and John, forgotten until now, and possibly the official win-ners, cruised past in the wooden boat, paddling with their hands, and reminded us that we'd better come in for tea before we all turned blue.

As the only girls in the party, Kate and I were given the privilege of changing by the fire in the boathouse first. As Viv had said – rubbing down by the fire was a real luxury. Joe and Josh brought the boats in as we found our places round the table, leaving the chair at the head for Joe.

It's a cliché, but food never tastes so good as when you're really hungry and it's eaten in the open air. Viv had gone to town with quiches and pizza as well as sandwiches. There was ice-cream in the cool bag. And of course there was my chocolate birthday cake. John Rowlinson made us all wash out our tea mugs before making a little speech about a son to be proud of and pouring us some champagne. He had his own fisherman's cool bag clinking with the stuff. We lit the candles on Joe's cake and he duly blew them out after we'd sung Happy Birthday. He picked off the little figures I'd moulded and wrapped them carefully in kitchen paper before cutting the raft into slices. 'Good cake, Charl,' said Ollie. 'I said you were good on the pie front.'

'Yeah, good cake,' said Josh, though he was mostly taken up with marvelling at Kate's ability to smear chocolate buttercream all over her face.

'No one's ever made me such an excellent cake before,' added Joe between mouthfuls, and the adults all started talking at once to cover up the implications of this last remark and the absence of Joe's real mother from his birthday celebrations. They were also tucking into the champagne in a big way.

'Am I going to be the only sober driver this evening?' asked Josh.

'Nah,' said Viv lazily. 'A little snooze in the sunshine after this lot and we'll all be fine.'

I fancied a lie in the sun, too, especially when I didn't have too much embarrassing flesh on show. 'Mind if I lay my pallid body alongside yours?' asked Josh and winked at me as the grown-ups reacted in their various ways. Viv tried to catch my eye; Louise was tight-lipped and John, who didn't have a clue about any of it, muttered something about not crowding the young lady.

'Fine,' I said, winking back. 'As long as I don't have to apply the suntan lotion.' I stretched out like a cat on my towel, exercised, fed and now relaxed. Josh lay beside me and I sensed the band of heat that hovered between our bodies, but it didn't do anything to me now. I drifted into a doze, lulled by the distant sounds of the other kids racing around through the woods in a wide game.

I surfaced when I became aware of a totally different band of heat coming from a body stretched out on my other side – and this time it was thermo-nuclear heat! I opened my eyes a slit to check who it was and found I was looking into a brown-eyed gaze that seemed to swallow me up. 'Didn't want to wake the Sleeping Beauty. Mind if I lie here?' asked Joe, never shifting the gaze. I thought I'd better play the sleep trick.

'Course not, birthday boy,' I said drowsily, and rolled to face the other way. The electric charge was tangible. I swear I could feel every hair and curve of his body across the distance between us. I felt as if I was on fire. I hardly dared move in case our bodies inadvertently collided and caused an explosion. Meanwhile, on the other side, Josh's marmoreal figure rose and fell as he breathed gently in his sleep and had no effect on me whatsoever. What fickle creatures we are, eh? Does this particular roller coaster never grind to a halt?

You can't sunbathe for long in the Lake District.

Soon there was a move to start packing up and take the younger children home to bed.

'We don't have to come now, do we?' said Ollie, nudging Joe. 'There's still a fire in the boathouse – it's a pity to waste it.'

'I can drive the rest of us home,' said Josh.

The others left eventually and it became clear that Ollie's request wasn't altogether innocent. 'I nabbed a bottle of champagne,' he said. 'Let's go out on the raft one more time and then come back to the boathouse and drink it. It is a birthday celebration after all.'

'I'm not sure I approve of this,' said Josh, and then when Ollie's face fell – 'Yes, let's!'

The raft accommodated the four of us very comfortably. Joe punted while the rest of us just sat and dabbled our hands in the water. I gradually noticed that a spirit of mischief was afoot among the boys. Josh and Ollie were exchanging glances behind my back. Was it possible that there was some unfinished Water Warriors business? Suddenly I was being lifted bodily and hurled into the water, fully clothed. I should have guessed. I thought I'd scare them, the rats. I swam out of sight under water for a bit. Then I surfaced, glugged and yelled and went under again. It worked a treat. Before you could say 'knife' Joe was striking out towards me in full lifesaver fashion. Mmm, this could be good, I thought. I waited until he was right by me and then grinned at him.

'Let me rescue you anyway,' said Joe. 'Birthday treat?' I wasn't complaining. We all reached the bank at about the same time. Josh and Ollie looked sheepish, especially when they saw I didn't have a change of clothes, and I stood there dripping and shivering.

'We've got towels,' said Joe.

'I've got a dry pair of shorts,' said Ollie.

They all sniggered for a bit.

'You can have my T-shirt,' said Joe. 'I've still got my shirt.'

'And my jersey,' said Josh.

'That's settled then,' said Joe, reaching for his T-shirt from the raft. 'Go and change by the fire. We promise not to look.' And they all sniggered some more, rotten lot.

It was lovely in the boathouse. I peeled off my wet clothes, praying the boys wouldn't come in (they didn't). I dried myself off and pulled on Ollie's gi-normous shorts. Then I put on Joe's T-shirt. It smelt lovely – I was reminded of how wonderful his hair smelt when he'd brought Scrappy home. But they were knocking exaggeratedly on the door now and coming in. I put on Josh's jersey.

'Snug as a bug in a rug?' asked Ollie, and proceeded to work the top off the champagne. Josh didn't have any because he was driving. We three, I'm ashamed to say, got very tiddly very quickly as we sat round the dying fire.

'It's been a good birthday,' said Joe, slurring his words on purpose.

'Marvellous,' said Ollie.

'Time for bed, said Zebedee,' said Josh. He gathered up the remaining things and gave them to us to carry to the Beetle. I stayed till last with Joe as he kicked the embers before putting a stone over them. 'You still haven't told me what you want for a present,' I said, as the last of the firelight flared in his face.

He stood over me for a second and started to reach out his hand. But he checked himself and looked down at me. 'There are a thousand things I could think of right now.' His voice came from the glowing shadows of the boathouse. 'But I don't think any of them would be appropriate for my brother's ex-girlfriend.'

Josh called us. Ollie sat in the front with him. I sat silently in the back with Joe and tried to keep my distance, too afraid of my feelings if I didn't.

On our return I had a brief moment with him. 'I've thought,' he said. 'Ollie was going to do a walk on the other side of Windermere with me on Friday, but he'd never make it with his ankle. Would you come instead – your presence as a present?'

Well, it wasn't quite what I'd expected, and long hikes aren't exactly my idea of fun. But when Joe treated me to another of his melting looks and my insides turned to water, I felt bound to say 'Yes.'

Fourteen

The day of the big walk dawned disappointingly grey, with rain a strong possibility, so there I was in a hideous blue cagoule over a sweatshirt over a T-shirt. I wore my jeans but had a pair of shorts in my backpack. The finishing touches were Viv's walking boots and some hairy socks. Had I been intending to seduce Joe (perish the thought), I couldn't have chosen a less likely outfit. Except of course, that it matched his. His cagoule was orange, though. (Aaaagh!) I was extremely glad none of my friends could see me. Hannah might have sympathised but the appalling vision I presented would have had Maddy and Sophie rolling in the aisles.

We set off for the bus stop in silence. I felt strangely shy now that we were alone together. Joe was very formal, and pointed out sights and land-marks for me as the bus trundled along the road to the Windermere ferry. On the other side of the lake we stood for a few minutes, in our cagoules, while Joe solemnly consulted the map. I wanted to giggle, say something that would bring us back to being Joe and Charlotte wearing silly clothes, but I couldn't think of anything. Oh well. Give it time, I thought.

The weather improved as we climbed. It was hard going for a slob like me, though I could see how amazingly fit Joe was. It was no effort to him at all. He gallantly offered his hand when we climbed over stiles, but looked away as I jumped down if I took it. We finally made it to a ledge high above the lake. I was sweating like a pig. 'Do you want to stop for a drink?' he asked. 'I could do with one.'

We sat on a rock below a stand of trees. The sun came out, and the view over the lake to the surrounding fells was spectacular. I took off my cagoule and my sweatshirt and stuffed them in my backpack. Joe did the same. 'Phew, that's better,' he said, and, for the first time, smiled at me. He lay back and stretched out in the sun, the gold streaks in his hair just like the model I'd made, gold hairs glistening on his tanned muscular arms. I lay back too.

'Look at the clouds,' he said pointing upwards. Piled white clouds cruised overhead. 'There's one that looks just like America on its side. Can you see it? That's north and that's south. And there's the West Indies.'

I have a pretty feeble imagination when it comes to clouds. 'That one looks like a sheep, no, two sheep – and a lamb . . .'

'And here comes Scrappy,' said Joe. It was true. The cloud looked like a fluffy white Scrappy bounding along (though the Scrappy we had fetched from the vet the night before could only limp on three legs). 'I could watch these clouds for hours,' he said. 'They change all the time.' He sat up. 'Epic scenery, eh? Though it's even better when we get out on the fells. You feel on top of your own world up there. Come on. We'd better keep moving. Long way to go yet,' and he hauled me to my feet.

He wasn't joking. The path led down through several more fields before we started to climb seriously again. I plodded along behind him and began to see the point of comfortable shoes and clothes you could take off. We didn't talk much. Joe was relaxed now, and no longer formal, but we needed our energy for walking. It was a very companionable silence, the rhythm of our stride broken only occasionally when Joe pointed out a hawk, hovering, or a rare wildflower, or a new peak as it rose up ahead of us.

As we got higher the scenery changed. There were rocks instead of trees, grey instead of green. Stretches of honey-smelling heather bordered the path and the grass became golden and springy underfoot. 'Another half hour,' said Joe. 'And then we *will* be on top of the world and we can have lunch.'

In all the years I've been coming here I've never done a walk like this. Can't think why. Probably because of Tom and Ned. 'I'm really glad you made me come on this walk, Joe. It's like heaven up here,' I said, when we finally flopped on to the ground.

Joe stopped in the middle of unpacking the lunch and looked at me. He drew a breath as if to say something, and then changed his mind. 'It *is* heaven,' he said. 'Especially today.' He left me to ponder that one while he busied himself with the food. Louise had done us what Joe called a fisherman's packed lunch. Viv and I slung things together any-old-how, but today everything came in watertight packages: savoury sandwiches, sweet sandwiches, apples, chocolate, fruitcake. 'Your cake's better,' said Joe.

After lunch we lay out under the sky. One or two walkers passed and greeted us, but mostly it was just us and the birds and the heather and the sun – bliss. Joe and I chatted lazily about this and that, nothing significant. Sometimes I turned my head towards him and found him looking at me and smiling as I spoke, but nothing more. I felt outrageously happy being on top of the world with him.

More clouds were starting to gather and build on the horizon when we stood up and shook the crumbs off our clothes. 'Better keep our stunning cagoules near the top,' said Joe. 'Looks like we might be needing them. Do you want to see where we are on the map?' He pointed out where we'd walked and how far we had to go to get back to Windermere. It didn't look far on the map, but I felt as though I had crossed continents.

We fell into our stride again as we trekked across the fell. The path started to drop and we made our way down through bushes and rocks, sheep occasionally straying in our way and bleating as they fled. Clouds started to cover the sun, but we were warm from walking, so we didn't mind. Sometimes the path was just scree and we slipped and slid, shrieking as we went. Other times the stream ran alongside and we splashed our hot faces. As we got lower, the shade of the mountains closed in on us and the mood felt different, less carefree. 'Pit stop,' said Joe. We found a rock to sit on and drank tea from the Thermos. He had cut his hand while we were sliding over the stones. I saw the blood as he handed me the mug. 'That looks painful. You should wash it next time we get to the stream.'

'Good old Charlotte. I love the way you're so motherly!'

I made as if to punch him. 'Gee, thanks. You really know how to make a girl feel good.'

'I mean it—' he ducked away. 'I do. I like the way you look after everyone – Ned, Kate, Scrappy, Viv.' He paused. 'Josh.'

'Well it's not something I'm proud of. I want to be – cool. Sexy. Not *motherly*!'

'Forget I said it. It was *meant* as a compliment.' Joe slung out the slops from his mug. 'Let's head on down and I'll wash my wounds.'

Soon after that it started to rain. We put on our cagoules and laughed at each other. We were still in high spirits when I slipped and fell in a gulley. Joe helped me up. I held on to his hand as we carried on walking. It was a strong, warm, dry hand. But without saying anything, Joe let go. I felt stupid.

He walked on silently. We reached the ferry, but

the boat was still on the other side. I bought us each a drink and some crisps at the mobile café and sat down opposite Joe, on the wall in the rain. I couldn't think of anything to say.

'It's been a brilliant day,' he said after a while. 'Shame it's nearly over.'

'I know. I don't feel quite ready to face all the others yet. Let alone my sister! She's probably there already!'

All too soon the ferry reached our side, and before long we were on the bus heading for home. It was still raining as we trudged down the lane to the house, cagoules on, hoods up. My time alone with Joe was so nearly at an end. I had to say something. At the bend in the lane I pulled him in, under a tree. I took a deep breath.

'Joe, just tell me – so I know it's not all in my fevered imagination – there have been so many times today when I felt – when I thought that you were going to, you know, do something or say something to me – but you always pulled back. Have I done anything wrong?'

Joe leaned against the wet bank and made me sit next to him in the rain. It streamed down our faces as he talked. 'OK. I'll tell you. Of course you haven't done anything wrong! But you know, all those years you fancied Josh – and everyone knew? Well, all that time, I was besotted with you, right? It was my secret. No one knew. I didn't want anyone to know. You seemed so pretty and so kind and I never thought you'd even notice me. And then, this year, the night when we were looking after Scrappy, it seemed like all my fantasies were coming true. When you hugged me, I was on cloud nine. But then, in the morning, everything was different. Suddenly you were going out with Josh. I couldn't believe it! I could see that you weren't even happy – it was so unfair.'

I was going to say something about Josh but Joe carried on. 'If we got together after all this time, it might be like you and Josh. I don't know if *I* could handle it. And what if it all went horribly wrong? Three days ago, you were still going out with my brother. How can I be sure you won't want him back? He's older. He's better looking!'

Rain was clinging to those fabulous eyelashes. I took his cold, wet hands and held them both in mine. I looked up at him. 'I won't hurt you Joe. I promise. I really wish I hadn't had that thing with Josh. It was all so stupid. But I can't bear for us never to be alone together again. It was too nice, too special.'

'It was, wasn't it?' He grinned at me and then, quickly, so fleetingly I barely knew it had happened, placed a gentle, rainwashed kiss on my lips. I was still registering the aftershock when he stood up and walked on down the lane.

I followed, just a little more hopeful than before, to where I knew Michelle would be waiting.

Fifteen

'Bottie!' There was a tremendous squeal as we were washed up, dripping, in Viv's kitchen. (Maybe I haven't mentioned my sister's charming pet name for me.)

Michelle was about to hug me, but she stood back abruptly. 'Ugh! You're all wet! What have you been doing?'

Viv stepped in before I even had a chance to say hello. 'Go and get out of your wet things immediately, you two. Joe – Louise's been fretting so you'd better get on home. Come over later if you want – Josh is. Charlotte, I've put your washed jeans and T-shirts in the airing cupboard – so you can change into something warm. Michelle can help me serve the supper.'

I hadn't realised quite how wet I was, but I certainly didn't feel cold as I climbed the stairs. Joe was gone before I'd said goodbye and there was a vision in the kitchen that was my sister. As I had stood there making puddles in my cagoule and sopping wet jeans and walking boots, Michelle had most definitely taken centre stage in her white strappy top and extremely short cut-off jeans. Her skin was a deep tan and her hair was bleached white-blonde. Her make-up was carefully applied, I noticed, and quantities of silver bangles jangled on her wrist, taking the attention slightly, but only slightly, away from the little ring and chain that perched in her pierced navel, glinting among the expanse of smooth brown skin. I was already missing the blissful fortnight I'd had with no competition. But it was a long time since I'd seen her, and I was dying to hear all about Corfu, so I changed quickly into my dry clothes and ran down for supper.

'We'll start again, shall we,' laughed Michelle, giving me a sisterly hug. 'Wow! You look so healthy! All bright-eyed and bushy-tailed – you make me feel like some kind of sleaze!' She looked over to Ollie. 'And why didn't anyone tell me what a hunk cousin Ollie has become?'

Ollie blushed prettily and said something like 'I don't think "anyone" has noticed,' before being interrupted by Michelle asking how soon Josh was coming over. (Ha! I thought. Little does she know what I know . . .)

'We are going down to the weir after supper, aren't we?'

'Of course,' we all told her.

'Because I've got so much to squeeze into so little time. Viv reckons we should go into town for the market tomorrow morning, Charl, and perhaps somewhere touristy and lakesy in the afternoon. And then, as it's our last night, I'm pushing for a barbecue at the boathouse in the evening. What do you think? Do you think the Rowlinsons would come too? We can have a family picnic on Sunday before we go. That way I think we'll have just about covered everything.'

Phew! I'd forgotten what a whirlwind Michelle was. I always knew we were travelling in different lanes.

After supper she replaced her shorts with white jeans in deference to the brambles and wouldn't sit still until she could hear Josh and Joe's voices in the courtyard. They were preceded by Kate, who burst in to the kitchen where we were, saying 'Come on, everyone. We're all going down to the weir!'

'*We're* all going to the *weir*! *We're* all going to the *weir*!' sang Ned.

'And *Scrappy*'s going to the weir, too,' said Viv. 'On a lead. Can you cope, Charlotte?'

'Maybe I should take her,' said Michelle. 'Charlotte's not always very good with dogs, are you Charl?'

'I think you'll find that Charlotte is extremely good with this particular dog!' said Viv. 'Charl, I can't believe we haven't had a moment to tell Michelle why Scrappy has a bandage on her leg!'

'Silly old girl,' said Michelle. 'Did she fall down a rabbit hole then?' Josh came in at that moment. 'Josh!' Michelle coloured. 'Hi!' And she moved as if to throw her arms round him and go 'Mwah.'

But Josh stayed put. 'Hi, Michelle.' (He was

embarrassed, and so he should be.) He nodded to me. 'Are we off then?'

'Yes, yes, let's go,' said Michelle. We were all outside before she noticed Joe. 'Hey! And isn't Ollie's little friend growing up too! You'd better watch out Josh. You'll have serious competition soon!' Joe lowered his eyes demurely, but managed to give me a quick smile before pairing off with Ollie.

Michelle followed with a slightly nonplussed Josh. Kate and Ned scampered along after them, leaving me with Tom and Scrappy dragging on her lead. Tom held my hand (and I'd thought he might never do that again) and said, 'Isn't it great having Michelle here? It feels just like old times again.'

As on my first night, the rain had cleared to give a beautiful fresh evening. I felt almost as though I was being given a fresh chance at the holiday. It was as if the episode with Josh had never happened. And Joe was my secret. I knew better now than to make my feelings public.

Unlike Michelle. She was all over Josh. Or would have been if he had let her. I could see her working at it even from a distance. She flashed white and tan and jangly silver as she swayed along. From time to time I also caught her voice drifting over to where Tom and I were hauling Scrappy out of the brambles. 'Well Josh, I hope my little sister hasn't been giving you too much trouble this year when I wasn't here to protect you! . . .' And, 'Any chance of you and me slipping off to the pub tonight when all the younger ones are out of the way? I've got used to having a Bacardi and Coke at sundown.' I wondered when Josh would put her straight about what had really happened. I assumed he would. I assumed *someone* would, though I thought it probably wouldn't be me.

But when Michelle came into our room later that night – having persuaded Josh to take her to the pub – I realised that perhaps no one had said anything. She was obviously ruffled. 'Charl,' she whispered loudly. 'Are you awake?'

'Mmm?' I answered sleepily. I wasn't sure I wanted to hear what she had to say.

'How d'you find old loverboy Josh this year?'

'Fine,' I said warily.

'Well, I suppose he never really talks to you properly anyway. Too embarrassed probably – you making your cow eyes at him, – but with me, well, he's usually very friendly.'

(*Very* friendly by all accounts, Michelle.) I chose to let her rattle on.

'But, there we were in the pub, me all bronzed and irresistible, open to offers, you know how it is, and well, he just didn't seem to fall for it. Weird, because all the time we were in Corfu I couldn't keep the lads away. But Josh – well. And he is very attractive these days. I can see why you had a thing about him – I mean even *I* quite fancy him now. But he really wasn't interested. I tried to find out if he had a girlfriend on the quiet but he wouldn't tell me. Kept making jokes and saying sarky things, you know the way he does . . .'

I most certainly did. But I wasn't letting on.

'Still, I might work on him. What do you think, Charl? You don't mind? I mean, I know you're madly in love with him and everything, but he is more my type, isn't he?'

I kept quiet. In fact I pretended to be asleep, though inside, I have to admit, a small and rather unsisterly satisfaction was taking hold.

Saturday! Our last full day. I couldn't believe it. I so much wanted a bit more time with Joe on his own, but I had no way of telling whether or not I would get it, especially with Michelle here.

She was slightly calmer over breakfast, and I finally managed to hear about Corfu, though of course it was a fairly predictable saga of divine men falling head over heels in love with her. (I'd forgotten just how self-centred she was.) And we managed to tell her about the various dramas that had befallen Ollie and Scrappy. But still no one let on about me and Josh. I even began to wonder if anything *had* happened. Perhaps no one wanted to be the one to tell Michelle. Ollie, now very much in favour, wanted to stay there. For Tom it was all too painful and anyway best forgotten. And as far as the little ones were concerned, it all happened centuries ago. I thought once or twice Viv might have said something, but perhaps she reckoned that Michelle should hear it from me, if anyone.

We went to the market. It was good fun being with Michelle. She's impossible to ignore and she struck up conversations with people wherever we went. I was glad we'd gone into town, too. I hadn't been in as often as usual this year and there were all the usual places to visit – the river, the museum and art gallery for coffee, and the busy Saturday market – particularly good for jewellery and for fabric. We sifted through the silver rings and earrings. Michelle was looking at ear studs and new bits and pieces for her navel when I came across a tray of friendship bracelets. They had some made of plaited leather with initials tooled onto them. I decided to buy one with a J for Joe. I chose one that looked the right size. I could just picture it on his tanned wrist. After all, I never did give him a birthday present. I paid for it quickly while Michelle was trying on rings and shoved the bag in my pocket. I prayed I'd find a moment to give it to him.

We chose to go to Beatrix Potter's House for the afternoon. We crossed Windermere on the ferry with a million other tourists. Tom and Ned loved looking at the familiar pictures. Ollie was rarely far from Michelle's side, nodding agreement with everything she said. Viv caught my eye from time to time, and even said at some point, 'Thank God my adolescent days are over – how ghastly to be such a slave to rampant hormones. Not that I begrudge Ollie a little attention . . .' On the way home we had to wait for the ferry at the same little mobile café I'd stopped at with Joe. We'd both felt sad there before – only yesterday! – and today I felt a terrible pang at the separation that was to come. And still I didn't really know how he felt about me. I put my hand in my pocket and stroked the bracelet. Even if we didn't get a chance to be alone, I would still give it to him before we left.

Michelle, as you've probably gathered, usually gets her way. The barbecue was on and the Rowlinsons junior were coming. In fact they had already gone on ahead when we got home. There was a note stuck to the door that said, in childish handwriting: GONE TO BOATHOUSE – PLEASE BRING KETCHUP AND SWIMMERS. The boys raced around looking for towels. Michelle grabbed her minuscule bikini, 'Though I doubt if you'll get me into the freezing lake, not after the warm sea I've been swimming in,' she said.

I doubted very much that I'd be swimming either – a sunny day is one thing, a cool evening is another. But I hunted around for my swimsuit to put on under my clothes, just in case. I found it, a soggy bundle wrapped in an even soggier towel. Damn. That left my bikini. It had stayed in its bag until now. It would do for swimming in the dark, so long as I didn't have to stand next to Michelle. I put it on under my jeans and T-shirt and packed the last towel from the airing cupboard.

The others, including Scrappy, were piling into the Volvo. 'Have you all got something warm to wear after swimming? You might need something more, Michelle,' Viv regarded Michelle's midriff. 'Gets nippy around these parts in the evening. Not like Corfu!'

Michelle ran back up to our room to fetch a sweatshirt. She climbed back into the car with a sly expression on her face. 'Planning to give this to someone, Bots?' she asked me, holding out a brown paper bag. It must have fallen from my jeans pocket when I changed. 'I really think you should give Josh a break,' she added under her breath, and then, seeing the boys looking at her, changed the subject. 'Is Scrappy allowed in the water?'

I tucked the bag and its contents into my pocket again and heaved a sigh of relief. At least the others hadn't seen the bracelet. If Joe wore it they wouldn't know I'd given it to him. And Michelle obviously thought I still had eyes only for Josh. Best to keep it that way.

'I don't see why Scrappy shouldn't have a swim,' Viv was answering. 'She does love a quick dip, as long as you make sure she doesn't get too cold.'

We'd reached the lake. Viv waved us off. 'Have a good time! I'll be back for the little ones at eight. Look after them. Bye!'

The Rowlinsons had been busy. Joe and Kate had

lit a fire in the boathouse and Josh had a proper barbecue going outside. The burgers and sausages were laid out ready to cook and Louise had sent along some rice and salads and even some marshmallows for us to cook at the end. Michelle instantly offered to be Josh's assistant. Ollie went to help Joe with the fire in the boathouse and Muggins suddenly seemed to be in charge of the younger children and the dog. What a lot of difference the arrival of one sister can make!

Tom, Ned and Kate were determined to swim. They stripped off to their swimsuits before I had time to persuade them to reconsider. In fact it wasn't particularly cold yet. I launched the wooden dinghy with both paddles and climbed into it. That way I could supervise the kids in the water without getting wet. Soon the three of them, and Scrappy, were swimming. There were a few shrieks as warm bodies became immersed in cold water, but it wasn't as icy as the mountain water. They threw a ball for Scrappy, who swam to fetch it. She swam strongly and was less lame in the water than out of it. After a while I shouted to Ollie and Joe to call her in. 'Can you dry her off – keep her warm?'

'Use my towel,' said Michelle. 'I *won't* be going in the water.'

'Won't you?' said Josh, with one of his leers. 'That's a shame.' I could see Michelle wavering ever so slightly. But then he said. 'Don't think I'll be going in either, somehow. You need to be under ten years old not to feel the cold.'

Ollie hopped over to get Michelle's towel. She pulled it out of her bag, scattering the two halves of her bikini as she did so. Ollie picked them up reverently and handed them to her. Clearly he, too, thought it was a pity she wouldn't be swimming. 'I think my ankle's probably playing up too much for me to go in,' he told her, and went to help Joe rub Scrappy down in the boathouse.

'The first burgers are just about ready,' called Michelle. 'Any takers?' The little ones splashed to the bank. I rowed in after them, and shooed them into the boathouse to change. Tom and Kate were fine, but Ned was blue and shivering. I wrapped him in his towel and sat him on my lap to rub him down by the fire. Joe was on his way out. He looked over at Ned cocooned in his big towel. 'Oh Ned, what a nice *kind* cousin you've got!' he said. I stuck my tongue out at him and he skipped out. Oh dear. *How* was I ever going to get him on his own?

We all sat round the table to eat. I ended up between Josh and Tom. Michelle squeezed in on the other side of Josh and Ollie manoeuvred himself to be next to Michelle. 'Ooh, got yourself a fan there, Michelle,' said Josh, enjoying the blushes that spread over Ollie's face.

'Unlike *you*, of course, I don't think,' Michelle flashed back, still angry with Josh for being impervious to her charms. 'You have fans who buy you secret presents . . .'

I inhaled sharply, only to be rescued from a surprising quarter. ''Course I buy him secret presents,' said Kate stoutly. 'I buy them with secret money from secret shops, so no one knows about them.' I saw Ollie start to relax and enjoy the show.

'And I buy secret presents, too,' said Ned, not to be outdone.

'No you don't,' said Tom – and the awkward moment had passed by. 'Anyway,' Tom carried on. 'It's our last night all together, which I think is really sad.'

I put my arm round him. 'I think it's sad, too, Tom,' I said, feeling my voice about to wobble. I buried my face in his damp hair.

'Oy, don't do that!' said Tom, wriggling away. 'That's soppy! Can I have another sausage, Josh?'

Kids! Don't you love 'em?

There was a toot from the road. 'Is it eight already?' said Josh. Viv had arrived to take the little ones home.

But Tom wasn't budging. 'Pleecase let me stay,' he whined. 'I had to go early last time and I didn't want to. And it's our last night. Pleeease.'

Viv looked at us. 'What do you think? Can Tom stay?'

Well, as long as Michelle and Josh and Ollie were still around, I frankly didn't care who else stayed or went. 'I'll look after you, Tom,' I said. 'But you could take Scrappy, Viv. She's worn out.'

'OK. Come on then, Ned and Kate and Scrappy. I've got ice-cream for pudding at home for you two.' They went without too much trouble, even Scrappy, who didn't have the prospect of ice-cream for pudding.

'Can we go out in the boat?' Tom asked me, as soon as they'd gone.

'Yeah, you two go out on the boat,' said Michelle. 'I've got this card game for four people that I want to play with the boys.' Honestly, I could throttle my sister sometimes.

Tom and I went out on the lake. The sun was setting and it was beautiful. And romantic. I heard laughter coming from the boathouse. In fact I was glad I wasn't there with the others. I felt that it was dangerous to be around Michelle when at any moment she could discover the truth about me and Josh, or inadvertently expose how I felt about Joe. And anyway, Tom, despite not wanting to be soppy, was slightly luxuriating in the sadness of our last evening. I said he always picked up on my moods. So we rowed around the lake, one oar each, the colours of the sunset dripping from them as they lifted from the water. The sun dipped below the horizon. My time with Joe running out.

There was a call from the boathouse. 'Time to go home!' shouted Michelle. 'There's this thing on TV that we don't want to miss!' Tom and I rowed in and beached the boat. Joe and Ollie had packed up the rest of the stuff (while Michelle had continued to flirt with Josh, I presume). Ollie was looking disgruntled, but he still hung around Michelle. Poor Ol. I forgave him all his taunting in the past. I really felt for him, though I couldn't admire his taste. Had I been this transparent with Josh?

We carted everything to Josh's Beetle and loaded what we could in the boot. Josh looked at us all. He looked at Tom. Tom was extra. 'I can just about squeeze five of us in with all this junk, but I can't fit six. Joe, little bro, can you stay behind like a good egg to clear up the last bits and pieces? I'll come back for you after the programme.'

'That's a bit unfair. He'll miss—' Ollie started saying, when somehow I found the strength to intervene.

'I'll stay with him,' I said smoothly. 'I've missed the last two episodes, so I don't care if I miss another. The fire needs to be kicked out and the boat put back in the boathouse anyway – and that's a job for two.'

'Are you sure, Charl?' asked Ollie, looking relieved.

'Always the helpful girl, my sister,' said Michelle, getting into the car. Ollie scrambled in after her. 'Come on, Josh, or we won't make it. See you later, you two. We'll pick you up in about an hour then.'

An hour. I had an hour.

We went back to the boathouse with our bags.

'Fancy another go on the lake?' asked Joe, as the others drove off. 'Its ace out there when it's getting dark.'

That suited me. Joe sat opposite me to row. We pulled out into the middle of the lake. The colours on the water were less spectacular now, subtler. Joe shipped the oars and the wooden boat rocked and drifted, blissfully. He squeezed my knees between his. 'Fancy a swim?' I hesitated. It looked cold. 'Come on, it's great swimming at night. Ollie and I do it often.' He looked at me. 'Got a swimsuit on?' I nodded. 'That's OK then. Ol and I go skinny-dipping but I don't think I know you well enough for that – yet!' I swooned at the very thought of it.

This was it then. My bikini was going to get its big moment. I took off my T-shirt and jeans at great speed and slipped over the side of the dinghy. Joe followed. The water was cold, but silky and wonderful, like the tarn had been. The sun had gone down, but a huge harvest moon was rising. Joe swam round me in circles. He disappeared under water and came up right in front of me. We trod water together, ripples spreading in the moonlight. He reached for my hands under water and pulled me towards him. 'If I hold you,' he said, 'we'll sink.'

'I don't mind.'

'Have you ever tried kissing underwater?'

'No, but I'm willing to try!' He put his arms round me and his lips on mine, and down we went.

We spluttered, laughing, to the surface seconds later. It was impossible!

'Again?' said Joe. It was one of the best games I've ever played.

Too soon Joe said, 'We'd better go in. I've lost track of the time. Chuck me the rope from the front of the boat. We can tow it in.'

We hauled the boat ashore and into the boat-house. The fire was still going. Our shadows were huge on the stone walls. Joe wrapped himself in his huge towel and stood by the fire to warm himself. I shivered, feeling self-conscious in my bikini, and delved into my bag for my towel. I pulled it out – Oh no!

'What's wrong?' asked Joe.

The last towel from the airing cupboard was the size of a tea towel. I held it up. 'This!' I said.

'Come here,' said Joe, 'Share mine,' and he opened his arms to draw me inside. He held me close and kissed me at last as we stood there by the fire in our wet swimming things, enveloped in his towel. I was completely intoxicated by the smell of the lake and the feel of his cold wet skin. After a while I pulled away to look up at his face. He smiled at me, and then all of a sudden his eyes filled with tears. 'I don't want you to go tomorrow,' he said hoarsely.

'Now you've started me off,' I said, and I was in tears too. 'I'm going to miss you as well. Come on, Joe, don't cry. It's our last night. Let's be cheerful.

Please?' I picked up my little towel to dab at his tears. 'This is about all it's good for!' He gave a violent shiver. 'Let's stick some clothes on. Here,' I rubbed his beautiful brown back and his chest (gasp) and passed him his shirt, 'put this on.'

I pulled on my big sweatshirt while he put his shirt on. He gave me a wobbly smile. 'Thanks – "Mum"!' I made to hit him but he hugged me to him again. Something in his top pocket dug into my shoulder. 'Ouch! What have you got in there?'

'You'll never guess.' He pulled out the little figure from the top of his cake. 'Close to my heart, you see!'

'Daft thing! Oh, I nearly forgot, I've got you a present.'

'Me? I thought it was Josh you bought secret presents for!'

'No, that was Michelle getting it wrong.'

'She's a bit of a pain, your big sister, isn't she? Bit like my big brother really. They deserve each other.'

I pulled the little paper bag from my pocket and handed it to Joe. He unwrapped the bracelet. 'Tie it on for me.' He kept his eyes on mine while I tied it round his tanned wrist. It looked as good as I'd imagined – as far as I could tell by the light of the fire.

'Michelle saw it when it fell out of my pocket. She thought the J was for Josh.'

'One-track mind, that girl. You don't mind keeping us a secret do you?'

One day I'd want to tell the world how I felt, but I didn't mind now, not while it was all so new. But then again, I was going home tomorrow, so nothing really mattered.

'You've gone all quiet. You don't mind, do you?'

I sniffed, and leant against him. I couldn't speak.

'Charl? I thought we were being cheerful?'

'What are we going to do, Joe?' I wailed. 'I've just found you, and now I'm going away.'

He stroked my wet hair. 'Don't think about that. I'm not, not any more. It doesn't get you anywhere. Tomorrow's another day, and all that. Everything changes, anyway. Who knows, you might meet someone else as soon as you get back. Things'll be different here, too. Josh will go. Ollie and I will go back to school. Kate starts in the juniors. Dad even talks about moving house. We don't know what's going to happen next, Charl.' He looked at his watch. 'And we've got precisely ten minutes before my brother comes to pick us up. So let's make the most of it.'

Wow. We did.

It was John who arrived to fetch us. We were listening out for the distinctive sound of Josh's Beetle, so we never heard John's car purring to a halt. We didn't know he was there until we heard someone approaching on foot. We sprang apart and busied ourselves gathering up the last bits and pieces and went to meet him.

'Well done you two,' he said. 'Very noble of you.'

We got to the car. John opened the passenger door for me. I sat in the front. Joe sat in the back. 'Josh was going to fetch you. But it seems that he and Michelle had a bit of a spat. Had to sort it out in the pub.' John turned on the car radio. He wasn't one for chat. I felt Joe's hand come round the side of the seat. I reached back and held it tight. We sat like that all the way home, silent and holding hands in secret. I gritted my teeth at the thought of having to say goodbye. How could I ever do it?

John drove as far as his garage and told us to walk up to the house while he parked. As soon as we got round the corner to the windowless side of the house Joe grabbed me round the waist and pulled me to him. We kissed each other fiercely. I didn't want to let him go. We heard John shut the garage door. Joe stood back and gently traced the lines of my face with his finger. 'I love you, Charlotte,' he whispered, and suddenly crouched down as John approached. 'We saw a toad, Dad. There, I think it's waddled off now.'

John laughed indulgently. 'That's my boy! I'm sure the young lady's not interested in *toads*, Joe! Come on you two. Let's get you both into bed. You're off tomorrow, aren't you, Charlotte? I've said I'll try and get them home in time to say goodbye. No peace if I didn't. My little Kate's going to miss you, you know. She's loved having a nice big girl to play with.' Luckily I couldn't catch Joe's eye right then, but he tripped and fell against me, accidentally on purpose.

'Ooops, sorry!' he said, frantically clutching my hand and looking into my eyes for the last time. 'See you tomorrow, then.' And that was it. We both went in our separate doors.

'Hi!' Viv's voice came from the other room. 'I'm on the phone, Charl. The boys are in bed and Michelle's out with Josh. Have a bath, if you want. There's plenty of hot water!' Phew. I was able to scamper up to the bathroom and lock the door. I looked at my face in the mirror. Definitely flushed. Thank God I hadn't had to walk in on Viv, or Ollie, or Michelle. I could just soak in a nice smelly bath instead. I lay in the water and thought of Joe. I tried to fix the memories. I was going to have to live off them for a long time.

Later I popped my head round the door to say goodnight to Viv and then fell into bed. It had been a long day.

Sixteen

'Charl! Charl! Charlotte, wake up! I want to talk to you!' Michelle was shaking me awake. Quite roughly. 'Why the hell didn't you tell me you'd had a thing with Josh?'

I tried to get my brain into gear. What was all this? It was after midnight. 'I might as well say why the hell didn't you tell me *you'd* had a thing with Josh.' That silenced her for all of two seconds.

'But *you*! I mean, I've made such a fool of myself.'

'That's hardly my fault. So who did tell you?'

'It was Ollie, when the programme was over. I got a bit fed up with him moping around all the time, so I said something like – "You're great Ollie, but don't you think there's a bit of a generation gap here?" and he suddenly came out with all this stuff. "Didn't put Josh off Charlotte did it?" sort of thing. And then Josh got all flustered, and said, "Not quite the same thing, Ol." And Ollie said, "No, even bigger generation gap." So I go, "Will someone tell me what's been going on? Charl's been drooling over Josh since time immemorial – so what's new?" "*I'll* tell you what's new," says Ol. "No, Ollie, if you don't mind. I think I'll tell Michelle what's new – and what's now old. OK?" Ollie was really upset and stormed out – as dramatically as he could on one leg – saying, "Well, you'd just better tell her everything, because if you don't, I will!" and slammed the door.'

Oops, I thought. And, poor Ol. He must have been sore.

'So Josh bundled me into the car and off we went to the pub. In fact we went to two pubs. The first one was that lovely old one with the big fireplace.

We went in there, and I'd just got settled by the fire, when Josh said, 'Sorry – this pub doesn't feel right,' and off we drove to the one we went to last night. He obviously wasn't going to say anything until we'd both sat down, so I just waited. And then he told me, Miss Bottie, that what Ollie had been referring to was the fact that the two of you had had quite a little scene going – cinemas, pubs, and quite a bit else besides. And that it was all quite public. Everyone *knew*! Except me of course.' She glared at me.

'It was all over by the time you got here,' I said.

'So I gather. What came over you? Josh too hot to handle?'

I was about to say yes, but then I thought – why should I go into detail? It's none of her business. So I just said, 'It didn't work out, that's all.'

'*Josh* thought it was working out fine. *Josh* is really upset that it's all over. You've really quite hurt him.'

That stung. 'That's just not true. Josh was really understanding. He told me that he was all right about it. In fact, he was looking forward to you coming, and the two of you carrying on where you left off last year.' I thought I'd throw that in.

'As if,' she said, rather sorrowfully. I looked at her. She was really cut up. She sat on my bed with her tan and her sunstreaked hair and her enviable figure, and wanted to punish me for what I did with Josh.

'I don't know what you expect me to do about it,' I said.

'Well, you might at least apologise for not telling me.'

'If it makes you feel better. But honestly, I just assumed someone else would. I wasn't exactly proud of the whole business, and it did seem to upset just about everyone. You obviously had the right idea last year, doing it on the sly.'

'Thing was,' she said glumly, 'I would have been quite happy to go public. It was Josh who wasn't. He didn't want to upset *you*. And that was last year. He's really fond of you Charlotte. But he says he just did everything wrong.'

What was Josh playing at now? The sympathy card to woo Michelle? I didn't know. I didn't want to know. I knew where my true affections lay. 'He's a complicated guy, Michelle. But I'm fond of him too.'

'Maybe you should let him know that. Did you give him the bracelet?'

Big change of subject needed! 'Do you mind if I go back to sleep now? Josh is all yours, as far as I'm concerned, apart from the fact that we're going on a family picnic tomorrow and then going home, so you'll see him for all of two minutes before we leave.'

She started to get into her nightclothes. 'Actually we might be seeing more of him if he gets the grades he wants. He's got a provisional place at UCL. Be good, wouldn't it, having Josh around to do things with? My friends would be dead jealous. You have to admit, he's a very fit bloke.'

Things were changing already. Just like Joe had said.

' 'Night,' I said. My real secret was safe. I could go to sleep again.

So. That's about everything really. We had our picnic the next day. The sun shone. We all swam. Scrappy stayed on a lead. (Joe is definitely going to train her, by the way. Viv, who I'm sure knows a lot more than she lets on, said that she thought Joe would need something to keep him busy when we'd all gone.) Michelle was particularly nice to Ollie. I could just see him blossom. It made me feel very old.

Michelle and I packed and then, just as we were leaving, all the Rowlinsons lined up to say goodbye. Kate leapt into my arms, saying 'Don't go! Don't go!' but both the boys were very restrained. Joe allowed himself to be 'Mwah-ed' by Michelle while Josh managed to squeeze me tightly and say quietly, 'I think I'll miss you more than you'll miss me,' and then more loudly, 'You might be seeing more of me than you bargained for if I get into UCL – keep your fingers crossed!' And then he turned his attention to Michelle. But I wasn't looking, because I was saying goodbye to Joe, and I was trying not to let anyone see that I was fighting tears. He held me round my

waist under my T-shirt and whispered in my ear –
instead of going 'Mwah' – 'I'm putting a note in
your pocket. Read it later.' And then he was gone.
He just turned and ran into the house. Our family
got into Viv's Volvo and drove to the station.

The train was hot and crowded. Luckily Michelle
and I had reserved seats. I was having trouble
keeping my face under control. 'Just going to the
loo,' I told Michelle, as the train got under way. Of
course there was a queue for the loo, but I didn't
trust myself to read Joe's message until there was a
locked door between me and the rest of the world.
At last I got in. I let the tears come as I unfolded the
little piece of paper. On it was a beautiful drawing of
a toad and the words written around it in a circle
were:

Remember what I said before we met this fella.
You are the sweetest, kindest, sexiest,
loveliest girl in the world.
Me and Mr Toad both think so.
All my love, Joe.
P.S. *Please don't change too much.*

OK, so I did something really corny. I stuffed the
note down my bra. Yes, next to my heart.

The picture had made me smile. I splashed my
face with cold water, took a deep breath and went
back down the swaying train to my seat.

Epilogue

The rest of the holidays were pretty boring. I slept in late, shopped, went to the lido, spent time with Hannah. I filled her in on most of what had happened, but I didn't feel ready to tell her absolutely everything about Joe. He was still my secret and I wanted to enjoy him alone.

All too soon it was the end of the holidays. The evenings were crisp and the mornings were dewy. Michelle's results were OK. Josh's were good enough to make him our neighbour – well, bring him closer, come October anyway. The end-of-holiday sleepover was at Hannah's because Sophie's family had only just got back. Hannah had surprised us by really wanting to have it there. What's more, having threatened not to give anything away, she was full of it. After all, her new boyfriend lived quite near, and looked as if he was going to be around for some time.

Maddy and Sophie rolled up together. There's nothing like seeing those two for all my old insecurities to return. Maddy of course looked gorgeous, though I couldn't help noticing that her make-up was almost too carefully applied, as if to cover something up. The glow wasn't all good health and sun tan. Sophie on the other hand wore the shortest shorts possible, showing her long brown legs off to perfect advantage. Her hair had gone lighter in the sun and her face – was this possible – had a slightly softer, less angular look than I was used to. Hey, what had happened there, then? Perhaps she had finally discovered what it was like to fall in love with someone, rather than having them all fall in love with you.

Preliminaries over, we settled down to exchange our stories. 'Come on Charlotte. What about the lovely Josh? Did he fall at your feet?' asked Sophie.

I gave Hannah a warning look. 'Well, I suppose you could say that,' I said. And I told them all about Josh.

'And you didn't want to carry on?' asked Maddy, wide-eyed. 'A hunk like that? And him preferring you to Michelle. You must have been mad.'

'He's starting university near here next month,' I told them.

'What? Oh introduce me please!' Perhaps Maddy's holiday hadn't been as romantic as everyone else's. I would have to wait to find out.

'I think his younger brother sounded rather nice,' said Sophie thoughtfully.

Hannah cut in protectively. 'My turn now.' She smiled back at me. My secret was safe for a while longer.

Also in the *GIRLS LIKE YOU QUARTET*:

Four girls, four lives, one summer.

It was Maddy's idea that all four of them should have holiday romances and report back at the end of the summer.

These are their stories . . .

Sophie

Blonde, drop-dead beautiful Sophie is used to getting her own way, and not worrying about the broken hearts she leaves behind. She's determined that a family camping holiday in France is not going to cramp her style. What's more, she knows exactly who she wants . . . but does he feel the same way about her?

Hannah

Hannah is the clever one, and hard to please – but she's really shy too. She doesn't fancy her chances on a summer music course – so she decides that the boys are just not worth bothering about . . . not any of them . . . or are they?

Maddy

Finding romance has never been a problem for Maddy – she's always been a beauty, and dramatic with it. So she can't wait for her exotic holiday in Barbados with Dad – it's going to be brilliant, and so different from life at home with impoverished Mum. The stage is set – but is romance all that lies in store for Maddy?